# THE
# RAFT

ALSO BY S. A. BODEEN

*The Compound*

*The Gardener*

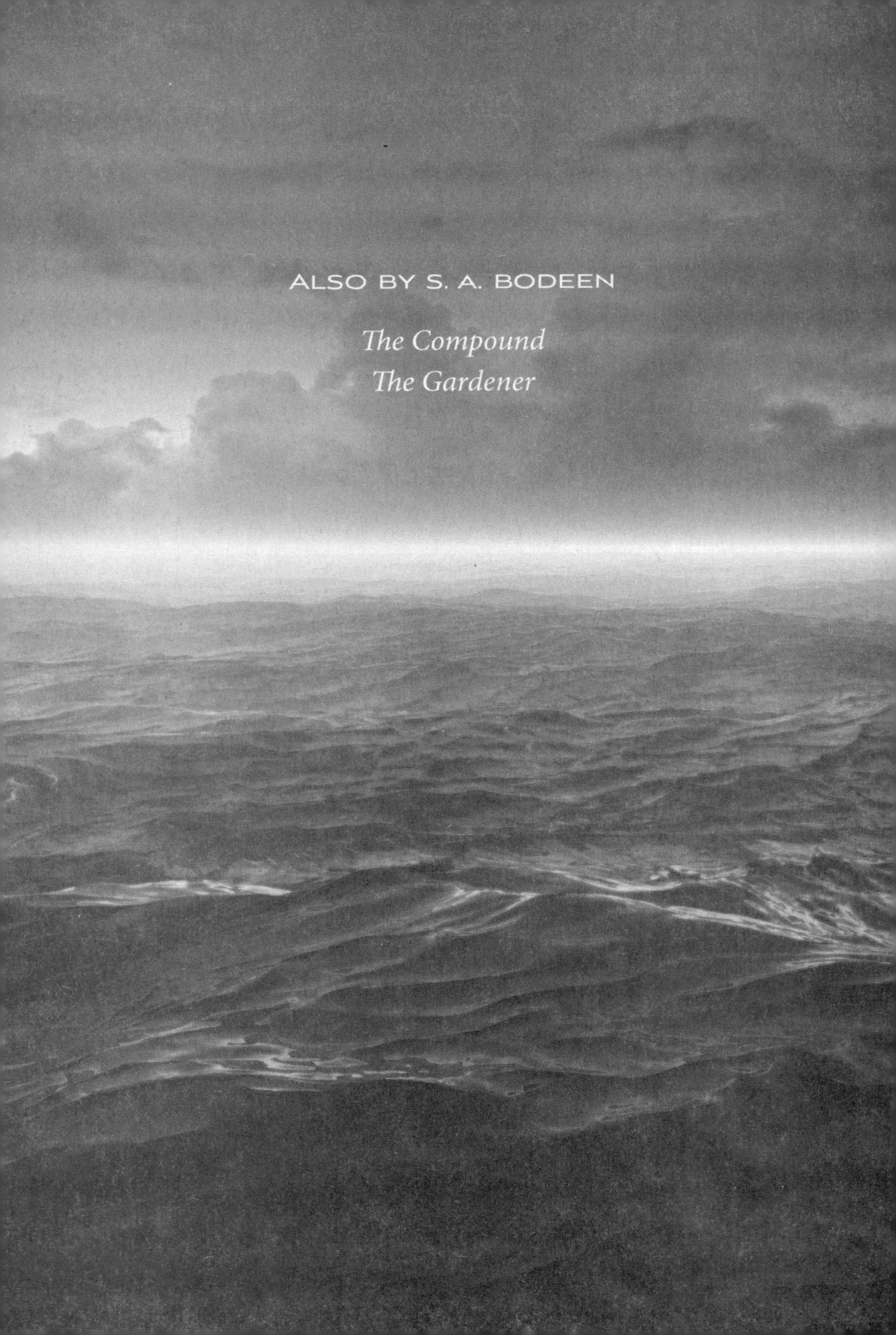

# THE
# RAFT

S. A. BODEEN

FEIWEL AND FRIENDS

NEW YORK

*For Tim,*
*and everyone else who ever took*
*that flight to Midway . . .*

A FEIWEL AND FRIENDS BOOK
An Imprint of Macmillan

THE RAFT. Copyright © 2012 by S. A. Bodeen. All rights reserved. Printed in the
United States of America by R. R. Donnelley & Sons Company, Harrisonburg,
Virginia. For information, address Feiwel and Friends,
175 Fifth Avenue, New York, N.Y. 10010.

Library of Congress Cataloging-in-Publication Data Available

ISBN: 978-0-312-65010-0

*Book design by Ashley Halsey*
*Feiwel and Friends logo designed by Filomena Tuosto*

First Edition: 2012

10 9 8 7 6 5 4 3 2

macteenbooks.com

*To survive it is often necessary to fight and to fight you have to dirty yourself.*

—George Orwell

# one

The dude with the lime-green Mohawk and dark wooden plugs in his earlobes looked down at me, the long silver needle in his rubber-gloved hand pointed directly at my face.

"Wait." I swallowed and gripped the arms of my chair.

Jutting out one hip, he rolled his eyes. "Do you want your nose pierced or not?"

"Yes, just . . . can you tell me something worse?" I pointed at the needle. "Something that is worse than that?"

He probably thought my request was insane, but that was how I coped with unpleasant things. Once I found out something worse, then it was easier to deal with. Whether it was a filling at the dentist or an end-of-term physics test, finding out things that were worse helped me deal with new challenges.

Green Mohawk Dude seemed to think about it as he looked around. A blond pregnant woman in tall suede boots and a fuchsia halter dress browsed through the gold hoops. With one gloved finger, he pointed at her. "Childbirth. Fairly certain that hurts worse."

"I'm fifteen." My turn to eye roll. "Something a little more relative? Not so obviously inappropriate?" I got ready to leave.

He pointed down at his black flip-flops. "See my big toes?"

My glance went downward and I flinched. His toes were big and callousy with yellowish nails. Easily the ugliest toes I'd ever seen.

*Sick.*

Green Mohawk Dude said, "Last year I climbed Mount Kilimanjaro. Coming down, my toes got smashed into the front of my boots. Ended up losing both my big toenails. Took them eleven months to grow back."

I asked, "And that hurt worse than getting your nose pierced?"

"Guess so." He shrugged. "Now, can we do this?"

Nodding, I closed my eyes as he shoved the needle through my skin.

A rush of stinging flooded up my nose. "Holy crap!" My eyes watered so bad I had to blink like crazy, then I finally gave up and kept them shut for a while. When I did open them again, first I glared at the green-haired liar standing in front of me, then looked in the mirror to check out the diamond adorning my nose. "Sweet."

"No swimming in pools for a month. Even though they're chlorinated, they could have germs. And lakes, rivers . . . avoid those. The ocean too. Just to be safe. You don't want to get it infected." He handed me a plastic baggie with alcohol swabs and Xeroxed instructions. "So now you can go back to the mainland with the new look you got in Honolulu."

"Um, yeah," I said, suddenly wondering just how much trouble I would be in when my parents saw my nose. "Actually, I don't live on the mainland. I live the other direction, out on Midway Island."

"Midway as in the Battle of Midway?"

I nodded.

His eyebrows went up and he nodded. "Very cool. You're lucky."

*Lucky.*

If I had a dollar for every time someone called me that, I'd be rich, because that's all I heard when I told people about my life.

When I told them that I lived on a coral atoll in the middle of the Pacific:

*Lucky.*

When I told them that I didn't go to a real school:

*Lucky.*

When I told them that I hung out among dolphins and monk seals and nesting albatross:

*Lucky.*

For three years, my parents had been research biologists on historic Midway, now a national wildlife refuge, so I lived there too, in the old admiral's home called Midway House. Sure, there were cool things like having my own golf cart and making my own hours for home school and getting to hang out with *National Geographic* photographers. Plus the fact I knew more about ocean fish and seabirds than most post-graduate researchers.

Those things did make me feel lucky.

But then there were other things that did not make me feel so lucky.

Like having the Internet crap out for days at a time, and not even owning a cell phone because there was no reception, and getting only three television channels, one of which was CNN, none of which were MTV. What's the point of even having television?

Not to mention being the only kid among fifty or so adults, which left me no one to talk to except for Facebook friends, and that was only when the Internet worked.

Lately it seemed there were a lot more days when my life felt less like luck and way more like suck.

I paid Green Mohawk Dude, tipped him a little, and then headed back for AJ's apartment.

What saved me from going crazy most of the time was Dad's

sister, my aunt Jillian, who lived in Honolulu. AJ, as I called her, had a place right on Waikiki Beach and was a consultant, which meant she got to do all her work from home. She was way younger than Dad, only about thirty, and when I couldn't take the isolation anymore, my parents would throw me on the supply flight returning to Honolulu from Midway and send me to her. And that's where I had been spending the month of June.

When I walked in, AJ was on the phone. Her long brown hair was up in a clip and she had a plumeria-laden cover-up on over her red bikini. AJ's eyes widened when she saw my nose, then she gave me a thumbs-up. As soon as she hung up, she came over and grabbed my chin, eyeing my new piercing. "Let me see this diamond I paid for." She grinned. "Your parents are never going to let you come here again."

I tossed my green crocheted purse on the table. "I'm getting my suit on."

AJ spent every day sitting by the pool with me, although she did try to get me to branch out. She called through the bathroom door: "Can't we do the beach today, Robie? We can get a good spot by the Hilton."

"Nope." I put on my purple cheetah bikini. "Two words. *Sand* and *waves.*"

She laughed. "For someone who lives on an island, you are the most ocean-aversive person I've ever met."

"I love the ocean!" I protested, as I opened the door.

AJ groaned. "You just don't like to touch it."

"Exactly. I just like to look. " I pointed at my nose. "Plus I have instructions not to go in the water."

She shook her head. "Finally, your perfect excuse to not get wet."

We went down to the pool. Wearing my contented smile, I leaned back on my pool chair and turned on my e-reader to Stephen King's newest, which I was almost done with. There was absolutely nowhere else I would rather be at that moment. "Now, this is the life."

She asked, "So what shall we do tonight?"

Every evening we headed off to do something, like see a movie or get pedicures at Ala Moana Center. My toes currently sported bright orange polish, rhinestone flowers on both big toes. One night my aunt surprised me by having a friend of hers come and give me cornrows. My dirty-blond hair was almost to my waist, so it took forever. When she finished, I looked in the mirror and tried not to show my shock. With my tan, the cornrows looked a little tacky. And I didn't look anything like myself. But I didn't want to make AJ feel bad, so I lied and said I loved them. My dad would like them, so I planned on keeping them until I got back to Midway, just so he could see. Plus it was kind of fun to walk around, feeling unrecognizable.

AJ waited for me to answer about tonight.

"International Market Place?" I suggested.

"Sure. Cheesecake Factory after?"

"Definitely."

That evening at the International Market Place, a collection of booths and shops selling anything and everything, I found a henna tattoo stand where a pretty Hawaiian lady, dark hair to her waist and three rings in her nose, beckoned to me.

I wanted a real tattoo, but my parents were already going to freak over my nose. AJ had signed the permission form only after I promised to take all the blame. That's how deep her coolness went. She had even sprung for the diamond, which, even she admitted, totally rocked. So, given I'd already used up my quota of quasi-permanent bodily changes my parents would dislike, I started to look through the book of henna tattoo samples.

AJ tapped me on the arm. "I'm going to be right over there by those shell planters."

The tattoo lady asked, "You want your aumakua?"

"What's that?"

"Your ancestral guide. The spirit that protects your ohana. Your family, yeah?"

"I'm not Hawaiian."

The tattoo lady smiled. "Mine is the honu." She pointed to a picture of a sea turtle.

"I love green sea turtles." I sat down on the wooden chair and propped my foot up on a stool.

With a little plastic bottle, she squeezed the brown henna out like she was painting, and it tickled my ankle. The henna turtle looked like brown mud when she finished. "It will dry, but leave it on, yeah?" She handed me a little baggie with a cotton ball inside. "It's soaked in lemon juice. Squeeze this on several times and the henna will last longer."

I handed her three wrinkled fives and went to find AJ.

There was a huge line outside the Cheesecake Factory, but I made my way through the crowd and inside the noisy restaurant where AJ was already at a table. We shared a slice of turtle cheesecake. AJ had just gotten a refill of decaf when her phone rang.

She glanced at her phone. "Barney."

Even I knew Barney was the guy who gave her the most consulting work. AJ always took his calls. "Hey, Barn."

I leaned down and touched my tattoo. The henna was stiff and felt like it was drying out my skin.

Back above the table, AJ's eyes narrowed as she listened for a while. "Seriously?" She listened a little more and rolled her eyes. "No.

No, that's fine. I'll come tomorrow." She hung up and put a hand on mine. "I am so sorry, Robie. I've got to go to LA tomorrow."

"That sucks." I wasn't looking forward to cutting short my trip and going back to Midway. But I saw her face and added, "It's only a week short, I was going back next week anyway." I took a sip of my Coke.

The waitress brought the bill and AJ got out her reading glasses. "You don't have to go back." She leaned forward like she was going to tell me a secret. "Bobbi can stay with you."

Stifling a groan, I faked a smile.

Bobbi was a friend of AJ's who lived on the other side of Oahu. We'd been up to see her a couple times at her beach house, which was always messy and full of smelly cats. Bobbi was old, like fifty, and had thick, waist-length dreadlocks and really tan, leathery-looking skin. She didn't believe in bras. Or deodorant.

"No, that's okay. I can go back to Midway." I paused. "Or . . . I could just stay at your place by myself."

She started to shake her head and protest, but I cut her off. "AJ, I'm almost sixteen."

AJ huffed out her nose. "Robie. You are not almost sixteen. You've only been fifteen for two months."

I shrugged. "Still, you have security up the ying-yang at your place, I know my way around . . ."

She looked at me over the top of her black cat-eye reading glasses. "Your parents would kill me."

"We won't tell them?"

AJ tapped the pen on the bill for a moment, and then pointed it at me. "Only if Bobbi stops in every day after work."

Ew. "Every other day."

Her voice was firm. "Every day."

"Fine." I held out my hand and we shook.

The next morning, after about an hour of instructions, admonitions, and warnings, AJ left for the airport. I was just getting ready for the pool when the phone rang. Bobbi said, "Hi, Robie. Jillian fly out yet?"

Technically not, since she was probably still sitting at the airport. "No."

"I can't talk, but can you give her a message for me?"

"Sure."

Bobbi's words were rushed. "I'm not gonna be able to stop in like she asked me to. My car died and I have to carpool with a guy from up here."

"That's okay." I smiled as I noticed AJ had left me a small fortune's worth of bills on the counter.

"Can she get someone else to check in on you?"

"Yes. Definitely. Don't worry about it."

I hung up. I was free for a week. Although I did already miss AJ, I did a little dance.

Free!

## two

Starbucks was on the first floor of AJ's apartment building, and every morning, I ran down and got myself a grande vanilla bean frappuccino. Before I went by the pool to read, I washed off the rest of the henna. The turtle was faint orange, but the lady had said it would darken.

And then I carefully doused my new piercing in rubbing alcohol.

The pool was lonely by myself, and I didn't stay as long as usual.

Back in AJ's apartment, I watched the rest of the DVDs from the final season of *Battlestar Galactica*. We didn't get much television on Midway, and I made up for it when I got to Honolulu. AJ had Netflix and I usually went through an entire series or two during my visits. Maybe it was weird, that I didn't get to watch television like other people, and I had to watch stuff long after it was on TV, but I also didn't have to wait from week to week to see what happened.

On the other hand, watching an entire series over a few days could be a letdown. Being so immersed in the characters and the story, kind of sleeping and eating them, it was even harder to come to the end, to know it was done.

The final episode had me in tears partway through, and I had to hit Pause while I looked around for some Kleenex. Finally, I had to settle for a roll of toilet paper and used up a lot of it by the time the episode ended.

I clicked off the television. My shoulders sagged and I sniffled and blew my nose again. I felt drained. I could always start the series over, meet Starbuck again for the first time, but decided not to.

For lunch I had some ramen noodles, and then walked down to Ala Moana Center. I'd been visiting AJ in Honolulu since I was eight, so I knew my way around. After shopping for a while, and scoring big on a pair of pink high-top Chuck Taylors, I headed back to the apartment, which was very quiet and empty.

AJ had several seasons of *Lost* on DVD, so I put on the first episode. The plane crash was a little intense, but I couldn't stop watching until the episode was over. Instead of watching the next one, a nap sounded good. When I woke up it was dark. I'd planned on running to McDonald's for dinner, but I didn't usually go out after dark by myself. But it was Honolulu, I knew it like the back of my hand, and McDonald's was barely five minutes away.

The tropical evening was warm and windy, and tons of people were on the well-lighted streets. Still, my heart pounded a little as I crossed the avenue. I'd never realized that I did everything in Honolulu with someone, either AJ or my parents. Come to think of it, everything I did, I did with someone. Even on Midway, when I was alone, people were never very far away.

As I got my plain cheeseburger Happy Meal and headed back, bag in one hand, vanilla shake in the other, I wondered what, if anything, I had actually ever done on my own before. A dirty guy without a shirt leaned against the traffic light as I waited for it to change. With my peripheral vision, I could see him watching me, and I shuffled away a little bit, trying not to be too obvious.

He yelled, "Lucy!"

The light changed and I stepped down into the crosswalk, walking fast. Just as I reached the other side, a hand grabbed a chunk of my cornrows and yanked.

My food went flying as I was whipped around.

The dirty guy stood there holding my hair, looking like he could barely stand up. "Lucy!"

My heart pounded as I tried to scream, yell, do something, anything to stop him. But all I could get out was, "I'm not Lucy."

"I told you to go home!" He grabbed my cornrows tighter, forcing my head down so I could only look at the ground where my vanilla shake had splattered white all over the sidewalk. "I told you to go home."

I tried to move away, grab my hair back, *something*, but he had a tight hold and was wrapping it around his fist.

I started to cry. "I'm not Lucy!"

*Why wasn't anyone helping me?*

Instead of letting go, he wrapped my hair even tighter so I had to step closer and closer to him. He smelled like fried onions and something else that made me cringe. Something gross.

A male voice shouted, "Hey!"

The guy let go and I stepped back. Another guy started yelling at the first one and I ran, the sound of pounding footsteps close behind me.

I sprinted all the way back to AJ's building, crying. The security guard wasn't there and I didn't want to wait in the lobby where someone on the street, maybe the dirty guy, could see me. So I ran to the elevator and punched the 10. When I finally got to the apartment, my hand was so shaky I had to hold it with my other one to reach in my pocket for the key. It wasn't there.

"No!" How had I lost it?

*Calm down.*

I took a deep breath, and then felt again. My fingers closed around the smooth metal and I breathed a sigh of relief. My hands were still shaking so hard I almost couldn't unlock the door. When I finally got in, I slammed the door, locked all three locks, and dropped to the floor, breathless. My back against the door, I hugged my knees and sobbed.

# three

No way was I staying there by myself.

Despite my initial excitement at being on my own, being free, I was done. I didn't want to be on my own. I wasn't *ready* to be on my own. More than willing to go back to Midway to be with my parents, I wiped my face and found my little calendar book from my bag.

Running my finger down the dates, it was clear I'd missed the passenger flight that went every other week, but the monthly supply flight left the next evening. Only one plane did those three trips to Midway a month, an aging Gulfstream turboprop. Unlike regular airline flights, the flights to Midway on the G-1 were pretty mellow. No security lines, no wait to check in, no worry about getting bumped. If you were a Midway resident, you could pretty much decide an hour beforehand that you wanted to go. Just show up with a passport, and they'd get you on.

I took a few deep breaths, just so my parents wouldn't be able to tell how upset I was. Then I picked up the phone and dialed.

I waited for the click, then the pause, then the ring. I envisioned our heavy old-fashioned black curly-corded phone sitting on the counter just outside the kitchen, could even hear the loud ring.

But there was nothing.

I hung up and dialed again. Waited.

Nothing.

Periodically, along with the Internet, the phone lines on Midway crapped out. They were all dependent on the satellites, and the wiring on the island was old, so it wasn't a surprise. Still, I wanted to talk to my parents, have them arrange the flight for me.

*Should I call AJ?*

I shook my head, answering my own question.

She would just freak out and feel guilty about leaving me alone. Not to mention maybe get mad at me for not telling her Bobbi wouldn't be checking on me after all.

Figuring I'd call Mom and Dad in the morning, I brushed my teeth and put on my pajamas. My room was down the hall from the bathroom. Usually no big deal, but I always had to pee in the middle of the night, and tonight I didn't want to go walking around when it was dark, and nobody was there but me.

So I went into AJ's room, which had an attached bathroom. I locked her door, tossed all her blue and green shams and decorative pillows on the floor, and crawled under the covers. The sheets were cool and I stretched out my toes.

Then I reached over to turn off the bedside lamp.

But I couldn't.

I did not want it to be dark. So I left it on and rolled over, facing the other way toward the sliding glass doors that went out to the balcony. The white curtains were shut.

Pushing the covers back, I slipped out of bed and tiptoed over to them. Reaching out a hand, I grasped the edge of the curtain. "One . . . two . . . three—"

I whipped them back, gasping.

Except for a few plant pots, the balcony was empty. And we were on the tenth floor; nobody was going to crawl up.

*Don't be a baby.*

I let the curtain drop. Still, I was relieved I'd checked.

I crawled back into bed, but I couldn't sleep. Without my aunt, my favorite place in the world had turned into something else.

I heard a noise. A tapping.

*It's just someone knocking on the apartment next door.*

The tapping continued.

*It's just something loose, blowing in the wind.*

*Tap. Tap. Tap.*

*It's the ice maker, something is just loose.*

But I knew it wasn't true. I knew it was the weird guy from the street, trying to get in, trying to get me.

I pulled the covers up over my head and trembled, my heart beating so hard I was almost able to hear it in the quiet room.

Now and then I peeked out of the covers at the glowing red numbers of the bedside alarm clock, which shifted slowly throughout the night.

*11:13*

*1:02*

*3:29*

I waited, ready for whoever might come in to get me.

*4:43*

Finally, just as it began to lighten outside, I fell asleep.

# four

AJ called at about nine and woke me up.

When she asked how I was, I lied, told her everything was fine and Bobbi had stopped in the day before. I felt bad, but what did it matter when I was heading home anyway? Then I tried my parents, but the phones still weren't working.

When I stepped in the elevator to head down to Starbucks, my heart pounded until I reached the lobby. The security guard who always smiled and called out "Aloha!" wasn't at his post.

Back upstairs, I packed, then went to the pool for a while, made a ham sandwich for lunch, and took a nap. About four, I got dressed. The drive to the airport, and waiting around there, would be hot, but the plane would be chilly, so I had my standard outfit for flying: khaki Bermuda shorts, a white camisole, and my green hoodie. I wore white flip-flops, but shoved a pair of socks in my bag. I debated adding my new Converse, but put them in my suitcase instead. Then I called a taxi.

As usual, the loading of the G-1 at Oahu Air Services was pure chaos, people hauling boxes and cartons and barrels out to the plane. I left my bags by the door to the waiting lounge and went looking for the woman who usually organized the loading. I didn't see her anywhere. A tall, bald guy held a clipboard, so I asked, "Where's Suzanne?"

"Sick." He shook his head. "Of all days. The Costco order didn't get delivered and there's a new copilot." He waved at a couple guys loading the plane. "Hey!" He headed off, leaving me standing there.

The pilot, Larry, came around the plane, wearing black pants and a short-sleeved white button-down shirt with gold pilot epaulets on the shoulders. Tall with dark hair that never had a strand out of place, he swaggered a bit.

I waved.

His forehead wrinkled for a moment, and I called out, "Hi, Larry."

"Robie?" A slow smile spread across his face. "I didn't even recognize you. Nice hair."

"Thanks. I'm trying to catch a flight home."

He nodded. "We'll be stuffed, but there's always room for you."

"I didn't see Suzanne."

He scratched his head. "Yeah, she's gone today. It's a mess, especially with communications down at Midway. My new copilot is around here somewhere, trying to make sense of it all. Max. He'll get you on the manifest. Why don't you wait inside where it's cool? I'll come get you."

The waiting lounge inside Oahu Air Services was air-conditioned and I dropped my bags, then plopped down on the couch. There was a little fridge near the seating area, and I pulled out a Coke, and then grabbed a handful of chocolate-covered macadamia nuts from the koa wood bowl on the table. A golf match blared from the television mounted high on the wall, but there wasn't a remote to change the channel, so I flipped through a *Glamour* magazine for a while.

The flight was supposed to be wheels up around five, putting us on the ground at Midway about eleven or so. During nesting season for the albatross, the Midway runway had hundreds of thousands of bird crossings a day, potential disaster if a jet engine sucked one in, or even if the G-1 collided with a bird. Albatross weigh about fifteen pounds; they're like a flying cannonball with feathers. So flights could only land and take off there at night, when the birds were less active.

I never really got used to flying all that way over water at night. I wasn't scared, because I'd been flying since I was little, but I still tried my best not to think about it. Knowing Larry, and trusting him, helped a lot. I'd taken the G-1 back and forth to Midway probably twenty or so times, most of those at night. Larry could probably fly the route blindfolded.

I waited for them to come and tell me to get weighed. The G-1 could only hold 3,800 pounds of cargo and people, because that's how much it could still fly with if one engine went out. Since we got a supply flight only once a month, and that was all our mail, groceries, parts they needed for the generator and other equipment, it meant we did without a lot that was simply too heavy. Like milk. A gallon of milk weighed eight pounds, and milk for fifty people added up too fast. Thinking about it, I fell asleep on the couch.

Larry shook me awake. "We're ready to go." Then he asked me something about Max and weighing in and paperwork or something.

Still groggy, I just nodded. My watch said nine, which meant we were getting a late start.

He carried my big bag; I took my small one and my backpack. I climbed up the short flight of steps and ducked my head as I stepped aboard. All nine rows of the red upholstered seats were chockful of boxes and cargo, except for two seats halfway back, right next to the starboard exit. The new copilot was already up in the cockpit. Max looked about twenty-five or so; I couldn't tell. Younger than AJ anyway. His dark hair was very short, like in the military, and he wore the same black pants and white shirt as Larry, only he also sported a black tie. Max glanced my way and didn't say anything.

I smiled. "Hi."

For about a millisecond, he nodded and smiled, but his eyes didn't. They seemed sad.

My dad was tall and always had to stoop to avoid the ceiling, but I could walk normally, albeit sideways, through the narrow cabin back to the fifth row of seats. The bin above my seat was filled with a blue mesh bag of satsuma oranges, my favorite. I noticed the Sharpied *Mitchell* on the label and grinned. Part of Mom's grocery order. I undid the top of the bag, pulled out two oranges, and then folded the bag and slammed the bin shut. The bin across the way was also stuffed, so I just put my bag in the seat next to mine. Then I sat down and buckled up.

Although Larry had said it numerous times, he gave me the emergency safety spiel, pointing out the exits, the compartment that held the emergency raft, the flotation device under my seat. He came across a little cocky, but I'd rather have a self-assured, ultra-confident pilot than an insecure one. As always, I listened, but hardly.

I'd heard it all before.

Larry went back to the cockpit and put on his headphones.

Not long after that, the propellers started to turn and air rushed out of the vent above my head. Sweat trickled down the side of my face, so I twisted the knob open all the way and held my face upward, smiling into the cool blast of air. Soon, the propellers buzzed and the plane moved forward, lining up for takeoff.

I looked out the window. A United Airlines jet rumbled as it lifted, probably heading toward the mainland.

A few minutes later, Larry's voice came over the intercom: "Here we go."

My knuckles weren't white as I grasped the seat, but my grip would definitely pass as tight. I wasn't usually this nervous, but I'd just watched the plane crash on *Lost* and was trying hard to put it out of my mind.

The engines motored up to full throttle as we stayed there, so it felt as if we were a dog on a leash, raring to go as someone held us back. My eyes went to the spinning propeller, already going so fast it was invisible, then to the words *Rolls-Royce* on the engine. Larry once told me that Rolls-Royce propellers went counterclockwise. Good *Jeopardy* question.

I leaned my head back on the seat as the G-1 surged forward, rocketing down the tarmac until we gained enough speed. The front wheels lifted and we were airborne, lights below us, the steady drone of the engines loud. Out the window I saw lights from ships in Pearl Harbor, then ships farther out, until they slipped away from my view, leaving only darkness beneath.

The G-1 flew steadily up until it leveled out and I relaxed to the familiar drone of the engines. Home was only a few hours away. Releasing my grip on the seat, I took off my flip-flops, put on my socks, and got comfortable. Still wiped out, I fell asleep.

When I woke up, my watch said one a.m. Lights glowed in the cockpit, but except for the small lighted track along the floor and the galley light, the cabin was dark. The ride was a little turbulent, but I'd been through a lot worse on other flights. An especially rough one had led my mom to say to Larry, upon landing, "Earned your money today, huh?" He had shrugged, then said he didn't think it was a rough flight at all. Since then, I'd read that turbulence didn't ever cause a plane to crash, so bumps didn't really bother me.

Five rows up, Larry sat in the cockpit and Max stood in the galley, sipping from a Styrofoam cup of coffee. Not as tall as Larry, Max was thinner, rather wiry, and athletic looking.

Max went back to the cockpit and Larry stood up. He got a cup of coffee, noticed I was awake, and came my way. "There's a storm front that moved in a little quicker than we expected. I'm going to skirt to the north a bit, but it shouldn't slow us down too much."

"Okay."

"Help yourself." He lifted his cup and went back up front.

Despite the late hour my stomach grumbled, so I unbuckled and went to the galley. A drawer held ice and drinks, and I grabbed a pink can of guava juice before rummaging through a big blue plastic cooler full of sandwiches. I chose a thick turkey one, and then went back to my seat. Unlatching the tray in front of me, I dissected my sandwich, taking off the tomato, lettuce, and white cheese before replacing the top of the onion roll.

At my first bite, the plane shuddered and bumped below me, and an especially large lurch shoved my stomach up into my throat.

Larry's steady voice came over the intercom. "Robie, make sure you're buckled in tight, it might get rough for a little bit here. We should be out of it soon."

I wrapped up the sandwich, saving it for when the turbulence calmed down. Maybe bumps didn't bother me, but I didn't really like eating during them.

As far as I could tell, we were only about an hour and a half from home. The ride got rougher and rougher, so that my knuckles were white as I held on and wished for Midway. Out the window were occasional flashes of lightning, but they didn't illuminate anything except for the rain pelting my window.

Constantly lurching in the dark, it was as if we were in a car sliding on ice. Leaning out in the aisle, I tried to watch the pilots in the cockpit, see if they looked especially concerned, but their backs were to me and their hands just looked busy. Larry hadn't announced anything for a while. I seriously wanted to call up to him, ask when we'd be landing, but it seemed stupid.

*We'll get there when we get there. Grow up.*

Then the sound of the engines got louder. I tried not to think about the dark and the water underneath us. Nothing but dark and all that frickin' water.

## five

Ten minutes later, although I wouldn't have believed it possible, the turbulence got worse. Now it felt as if we were in a snow globe that someone just shook and shook and shook. The lurching turned into deep plunges that made me feel like we were nose-diving, before we finally came back up, all the while bumping. One huge thump sent all the oxygen masks tumbling down, where they swayed from side to side. Mine swung right in front of my face.

Oh my God! Was I supposed to put it on?

A glance up front showed neither Larry nor Max had donned a mask. I couldn't very well ignore mine, so I tied a big loop in it, just to get the thing out of my face.

Another huge thump popped open a few of the overhead bins.

All of a sudden, a quick barrage of soft but forceful punches pummeled my head and shoulders, but the assault was over before I could even shriek or fend them off.

Oranges from the bin above my head.

One landed in my lap, and others lay all around me, rolling up and down the aisle with every shift of the plane.

I wanted to scream, but held it in.

Panicking wouldn't help anyone, especially not the pilots. Again, I tried to see what they were doing, their demeanor, their attitude.

Were they worried?

Struggling with the controls?

It was impossible to tell from my vantage point.

I felt an overwhelming need for reassurance, for someone to tell me everything would be okay.

That *I* would be okay.

But no one did.

As we bounced around, tears started sliding down my face. I stopped myself and wiped my eyes with the back of my hand.

*You baby.*

There was no need to cry over a little turbulence.

*Tons of things are worse than this.*

And then there was a hush.

Not totally quiet, but there was just less of a drone than there had been. I leaned over and peered out the window at the starboard engine. At the end of the wing, a blue light winked. Usually, the propellers were nearly invisible in flight, because they were turning so rapidly. But as lightning flashed, I could very clearly see the propeller, circling slowly, turning only with the movement of the plane.

That engine had stopped.

# six

Both trembling hands covered my mouth as I stifled a cry or a scream or whatever was making its way up. Two words whispered their way out. "Oh God . . ."

I wanted my mom or my dad or AJ or *someone*. I didn't want to be on that plane.

There was only one way to know the seriousness of the situation. I would have to watch the cockpit, see what they were doing.

Wiping my eyes on my sleeve, I prayed. *God, please please please let everything be okay. Please don't let us crash and please just let me get to Midway. And please let them be calm when I look up there.*

I leaned out into the aisle. From the back, the two pilots looked to be doing what they always did. Sitting tight. Focusing on the controls.

The loss of an engine had to freak them out too, right? Maybe I'd imagined it. I didn't know anything about planes, did I?

Maybe the engine was fine.

Again, I stared out the window at the propeller. Definitely not turning. Any idiot could see that the Rolls-Royce had quit.

But if Larry wasn't announcing anything about the engine, what else wasn't he telling me? Or was it not that big a deal? Airplanes lose engines all the time, right? I knew I'd read that somewhere.

That's why they load only 3,800 pounds in the G-1, so that one engine can still fly the plane. Only a few months ago, my dad was on a flight when the G-1 had lost an engine an hour after leaving Honolulu and they'd just turned around, no problem. After all, pilots are *trained* for bad stuff to happen, and maybe this wasn't even that bad. Maybe we were so close to Midway that they were already starting to think about landing, so why worry me with details about a stupid engine?

That had to be it.

We bounced again, hard. Beneath my butt, something in the frame of my seat gave way.

My eyes squeezed shut.

*Someone tell me it's going to be okay, please!*

How long could the plane handle getting beat to death like this?

The engine was probably the first thing to go, then a wing or the tail or some other vital thing that we need to land. Larry just didn't want to share the bad news.

I opened my eyes again and watched for some movement from the cockpit. Max got up. Bracing himself against the sides, he managed to make it as far as the galley.

*Was he getting more coffee? Things couldn't be that bad if he was getting more coffee.*

But, no, he wasn't getting coffee.

From underneath the bottom of the galley's shelves, he pulled something out and tossed it down the aisle in front of him. The cabin was still dark, and I couldn't see what it was.

With a foot, he pushed it along as he walked, until he reached me.

Now I wanted to scream.

It was a yellow raft. An emergency raft.

But we would only need that if—

Max reached beneath a seat, yanked out a flotation device, and shoved it in my lap. Then he uttered the first words I'd heard him speak.

Those words weren't *Everything is okay* or *You'll be okay* or *We'll be landing at Midway soon.* Instead, they were the worst words I've ever heard:

"We lost an engine and the hydraulics are acting up. We can't get out of the storm, so Larry is going to ditch the plane while he can still control it." He nodded at the flotation device in my lap. "Put that on."

# seven

My limbs froze and my heart pounded in my ears as I watched Max struggle to get back to the cockpit.

The flotation device was still in my lap, but I didn't even try to put it on. I couldn't make myself look at it. None of this was real, none of it.

Everything was fuzzy. Dull.

None of it could possibly be real.

The G-1 bounced all over, and then we went into a dive, so steep my belly strained against the seat belt, and then I couldn't do anything but hold my hands over my face and scream into them.

I didn't see Max coming until he was right there.

With one hand, he held on to the seat across the aisle. With the other, he grabbed my shoulder and shook, hard, until I stopped screaming. His face was inches from mine and his eyes narrowed. "Listen to me! If you want to get out of here, you have to listen!"

I couldn't move. I couldn't speak. I couldn't do anything *but* listen.

His breath smelled of coffee as he continued to yell at me, face-to-face. "The G-one should stay on the surface for about five minutes. If we stand any chance at all, we've got to get the raft out the window exit, then inflate it. You can't inflate it before it goes out the window, understand?"

He was so close, it seemed like I absorbed his words through my face, not my ears. I couldn't do anything but look at him.

Leaning back a little, he grimaced and then yelled, "Do you understand?" A few flecks of spit landed on my face.

I just sat there.

He slapped me.

Shocked out of my paralysis, I set a hand on my cheek and nodded like a maniac.

"Five more minutes and we're down. Get your life vest on; get ready to exit. We've got to be fast or . . ."

He hesitated, and then finished his sentence. "Or we'll go down with the plane. Understand?"

Again, I nodded, even though I only wanted to scream.

Max stumbled back to the cockpit.

I wanted so badly to hear what was worse than this. I needed to know what was worse. There had to be something worse.

Didn't there?

My hands shook so bad that I just sat there, cradling the one thing that might save my life. The one thing that would do absolutely no good if I didn't get it on in time.

Things suddenly got quieter.

Then there were new sounds.

Shudders and squeaks and an anguished mechanical groan like something out of a horror movie. Max barreled down the aisle toward me and, with a loud grunt, ripped the exit window open. The wind and rain burst in and would have nearly blown me away if I hadn't been strapped in.

But in one motion, Max clicked open my seat belt, gripped me under the armpits, and picked me up like a small child. Wobbling as the plane jostled us, he stepped to the opening.

The wind whistled and rain pelted my face. Putting up my hands to protect myself, I shouted, "My life vest!"

He just tightened his grip on me and screamed back, "Hold your breath and kick for the surface! The raft will be there!"

And then he threw me out the window.

## eight

The life vest was ripped from my arms as I zoomed through the air. The blast of wind and rain took my breath away so that the scream coming up from my gut stopped dead.

The falling lasted forever, my arms windmilling in the void. I wanted to stop moving.

Stop the noise.

Stop the wet.

Stop the cold.

Stop the blowing.

Stop everything.

*Stop.*

*Please.*

But if I stopped, it meant I was dead.

Dying wasn't what I wanted.

Breathing was. I just wanted to breathe.

*And live.*

# nine

My feet hurt when they hit the cold water, and I sank, feeling like I would never stop. Salt water poured in my open mouth as I screamed at the darkness swallowing me. I could see only black, could feel only the shock of cold and wet as I fell farther into the crushing nothing.

*Am I dying?*

Because if this was it, my last moments on Earth, I just wanted it to be over.

*God, please kill me already. This is more than I can take.*

ten

And I floated down . . .
　　down . . .
　　down.
　　It was over.
　　*I* was over.
　　Dying was so much easier than I ever thought.

## eleven

It turned out dying was too easy.

Something in me wouldn't accept the easy way out.

My arms flailed and my legs kicked, and after a moment, stopped my descent.

My legs kicked more and helped me move slowly toward the surface. My eyes were open, and through the blur, above me, reddish light glowed.

As I reached up with my arms, my air went. My panic grew. And I struggled to hang on; I struggled not to lose my mind. I struggled as if my life depended on it, because I was certain that it did.

*God, please, let me reach the light.*

*I want to live.*

Fighting with every kick, every ounce of reserve I had left,

the light got brighter,

closer,

and I reached up,

planning to burst out into the air.

But I couldn't.

I was at the surface, *I knew I was.*

But my hands touched a barrier. Something was there, soft and yielding, but I couldn't push through. The red was all around it.

I was so close, *so close* . . .

But something kept me from air, from life, from not dying.

In an airless, thoughtless frenzy, my legs kept kicking as my hands pounded, pushed, and slapped. My head whipped from side to side as I screamed a silent *no no no*—

## twelve

Suddenly, my hair jerked, and my scalp burned.

And then I was moving.

Up up up into the wind and the rain and the rushing and the terrible howling.

*No! You're hurting me!*

It was what I wanted to shout at the guy who attacked me in Honolulu. But there in the water I thrashed with my arms and legs, fought with everything I had as I choked, gasping for air. The hands were too strong, and they pulled me out of the water by my hair, until I fell backward onto something soft and wet.

I opened my eyes. There was only red.

And Max, on his knees, panting, holding a lit flare, the red light I'd seen when I was below. His other hand clutched hanks of hair, my hair.

Lying on my back, spewing up seawater, I was drenched and cold and shaking and exhausted.

I started to let fresh air into my lungs, but it hurt. It hurt so bad I didn't want to breathe for a moment.

I rolled onto my side, spitting and choking. I yelled at Max with as much strength as I had. "You threw me . . . out . . ." My words were weak, closer to a gasp than actual speech. "How could you do that?"

His back was to me.

Had he even heard my voice?

I sat up, still hacking into the deluge of rain and wind. I pressed my hands against my chest, trying to hold back the pain of breathing.

I couldn't believe how bad it hurt; how bad drowning . . . almost drowning . . . hurt.

Max turned left to where, about a hundred yards away, blue lights winked.

The lights on the wing. The plane.

"Larry!" Max screamed. "Larry . . ."

I had to cover my ears so I wouldn't scream myself. I closed my eyes and squeezed my hands tighter over my ears and was alone with the pounding of my heart.

Alone with the stinging of my scalp.

Alone with the pain in my chest.

Alone with the rain on my face.

Alone with my freezing wet clothes, clammy dead weight against my skin.

My breathing slowed.

Alone with the truth . . .

I had almost died.

Panic surged through my gut and I opened my eyes and uncovered my ears, welcoming the rush of noise and chaos, grateful for their distraction from the truth.

In the wind and the rain and the red-tinged night, the raft thrashed us up and down with no mercy. The blue lights slipped lower and lower until they winked out.

The G-1 was gone.

thirteen

Again and again Max shouted for Larry, screaming until his voice grew hoarse. Then he stopped and hunched over, hugging his knees, one hand still clutching the flare. The other hand held one side of his head.

Tears now mixed with the rain on my face, and sobs blended with my coughs. In a moment, my fear was going to overwhelm me, so I tried to cling to my fury. "You threw me out of the plane!"

Still not looking at me, he said, just loud enough so I could hear, "Would you rather still be on it?"

And then it was quiet.

He wasn't waiting for an answer.

Because any answer would have been stupid. Because by throwing me out of the plane he'd saved my life. And because I was suddenly certain he would rather be sitting in the raft with Larry instead of me.

What seemed like seconds later, but must have been several minutes, the flare went out with a little splurge of sparks.

# fourteen

Between the waves and the wind, the raft bounced about, giving us a ride nearly as harrowing as the one we'd just endured.

Shivering from both fear and the temperature, I huddled by myself, one hand clutching the slippery side of the raft, my other arm wrapped around my knees, face buried. I couldn't bring myself to raise it up, look around. I didn't want to know, for sure, that there was nothing to see because it was too dark. I didn't want to know, for sure, that I was stuck out there. In the nothing.

Was Max still there in the raft with me? He had to be. I told myself that, because I would have gone insane being there alone.

"Max?"

No answer.

Maybe he was upset, trying to deal with what just happened. Or maybe he hated me, not caring whether I was scared. And why should he? If I hadn't been there, if he hadn't had to take care of me, maybe he could have helped Larry. Maybe he could have gotten Larry out, and Larry would be sitting in the raft instead of me.

I lifted my head into pelting rain that stung my face. I held up a hand in front of my face. Nothing. A surge toppled me onto my side and I quickly sat back up.

I had to know that Max was there with me, but I couldn't bring myself to yell his name. What if he didn't answer? I inched along the side, feeling the raft as I struggled to hold on as it tossed about. I rounded one corner. Thinking he must be within reach, I held out my hand.

I would not survive this night if I thought I was alone.

My fingertips brushed his arm, found his wet hand. Chilled, dripping fingers closed over mine.

I gasped, mostly in relief.

Then he led my hand to a canvas handle, which I grabbed and held on to. His touch was gone. I wanted him to do something, put an arm around me . . . something.

Holding on tight to the canvas handle, I wrapped my other arm around myself and cried.

Eventually, my sobs became shudders. Then, when I'd run out of even those, I just sat there, shivering and wet inside the raft.

Something blue flashed for a moment. I blinked and wiped water off my eyes, trying to see.

A smudge of bright, glowing neon blue on the surface of the ocean, rippling and changing shape as the water moved. Phosphorescents. Algae, probably stirred up by the storm.

As quickly as the blue appeared, it was gone, leaving me wet and cold and in utter blackness. My shoulders slumped and I hunched back down.

I called out, "Is there anything worse than this?"

Max didn't answer for a moment.

Then, finally, he said, "Yes."

He didn't elaborate.

And I was glad. Because I didn't really want to know what could possibly be worse.

## fifteen

The rest of the night passed slowly, all wind and rain with the constant up and down. I clutched the handle. My gut churned and I leaned over the side and threw up. Half expecting the wind to blow my puke right back at me, I was relieved it didn't. My head pounded and my lungs still hurt. After puking the fourth time, I slipped my arms out of my sleeves and tucked them inside my hoodie, laid my head on the wet, cool, soft side of the raft, held on to the handle, and shut my eyes.

They opened to a dawn so gray that there was hardly a difference in the light. The rain and wind still pelted us as the raft surged down into large troughs and back up steep crests, but it was slightly quieter than before.

I must have fallen asleep, or passed out, because my neck was stiff from being in the same spot for so long. I sat up.

My clothes were sodden and heavy, and I shivered. The Northwest Hawaiian Islands, Midway in particular, were not all tropical. During storms, with heavy winds, it could be downright cold.

I stripped off my bedraggled socks and dropped them by my side. My fingertips were stiff and wrinkled, and I blew on them and rubbed them together to try to get warm. Slowly, I took in my surroundings.

The raft was bright yellow and six-sided.

Max's head lolled on the side of the raft and, with knees curled and arms crossed, he seemed to be sleeping. In that position he looked like a little boy. Some kind of yellow ditty bag was attached to his arm with a bracelet of blue bungee cord. I could see a white T-shirt through his drenched white pilot's shirt. One of his feet had a black sock, one a shiny black shoe.

Feeling a surge in my throat, I leaned my top half over the side of the raft and puked into the dark waves. How could there be anything left to come up? Turning my face upward, I let the rain clean me off.

A yellow-and-blue bag labeled "Coastal Commander" was attached to the inside of the raft, and I opened it up, hoping for some bottled water.

Inside were four flares.

Good, so we would have light if we needed it.

A little yellow cup.

For drinking?

I knew enough to not drink salt water. Or my own pee. Catching rain maybe? I held it up and caught a few drops, which I used to moisten my mouth, but anything less than a monsoon would take forever to fill the cup. I set it aside.

A small square mirror.

Signaling maybe?

Only if you knew Morse code. I hoped Max did.

As daybreak brightened the sky, I held up the mirror and looked at myself. The light blue bags under my eyes startled me a little, as did the glittery diamond in my nose. I'd forgotten about that. I swiped crusty stuff out of my eyes, then smiled wide and fake. Even in the middle of the ocean, my first thought was that I wanted to brush my teeth. Less than a day and they were already gross.

I put the mirror away and moved on to the next item.

A flashlight and some extra batteries.

I switched on the flashlight.

At least we wouldn't be completely in the dark anymore. Just knowing we had a flashlight, the ability to make the dark go way, made me feel a little better.

I switched it off.

A sponge.

No clue what that was for.

Seasick tablets.

Um, a little late.

There was a small first aid kit as well, with some gauze and bandages and a couple packs of Tylenol. My head was killing me, but I figured the Tylenol would come back up as soon as I swallowed them.

That was it. No food or water.

I zipped the bag back up and threw it at the side of the raft. Apparently, this kit was meant to tide you over while the Coast Guard was on the way, long before you got hungry or thirsty. How stupid to make a survival kit that didn't actually help you survive.

I glared at the kit for a moment, then sighed and reached for it once more.

Maybe I'd missed something.

Max stirred then, moaning and rolling over. A nasty gash ran from the outer edge of one eyebrow up his forehead.

I winced.

"Are you okay?" I waited a moment. "Max?"

He didn't answer.

I couldn't stand looking at that wound any longer and reached for the first aid kit. I pulled out a bandage and dabbed gently at his injury, wishing I had something to clean it with. "Thanks for getting me in the raft." I stopped what I was doing. "I thought I was going to die."

He didn't answer.

"But I didn't. Drown, I mean. We're in the raft. We're safe."

Swallowing the *for now* at the end of the sentence, I continued cleaning his forehead. I stuck on the adhesive bandage, and although it ended up slightly crooked, it seemed secure. "Not perfect, but it'll work."

I slid down and crossed my arms, leaning back on the side of the raft. My wet clothes were almost unbearable, and my teeth started to chatter.

I also had to pee. Bad.

## sixteen

I kept hoping for the sun to come out and warm things up. Warm me up. "Otherwise we'll have to add hypothermia to the list."

Why was I talking to Max? He couldn't hear me.

So I turned to the left and answered myself. "What list?"

Turning back to the right I answered, "Our list of issues."

"Like wet clothes?"

"And no food."

"No water," I added, looking around where there was nothing *but* water. "Well, no fresh water." Hearing the list out loud made it all real and made me worry.

I looked at his feet. "And one shoe. You only have one shoe."

Then I pointed at my bare feet. "One shoe is better than none."

I sighed.

Part of me didn't want him to wake up. He'd been so upset about Larry when the plane went down. I didn't know Max at all. I had no idea what he was going to do when he woke up. He was the adult in the situation. Whatever kind of person he turned out to be, I hoped he would have a plan.

We drifted for a while, and I didn't say anything else out loud. The joyless gray of the sky blended with the bleak darkness of the water. But I didn't feel as alone as I had in the dark.

And there was hope inside me. Hope that we would be found

soon. Being cold and tired and hungry wasn't going to erase the big picture. The big obstacle was getting rescued and I harbored hope that help was on the way.

Although I tried to think about other things, good things, things to keep me distracted, it became impossible to ignore my bladder.

For the first time, I was glad Max wasn't awake.

I did not want to put my legs—or any part of me—back in the sea. On my belly, I slid my bottom half over the edge. My legs were straight out, not in the water, and I managed to get my shorts and undies down far enough so they wouldn't get wet. Well, they were damp from the rain and seawater already. I didn't want to add pee to the list.

Emptying my bladder felt so good, I nearly cried with relief.

When I finished, I kind of splashed myself clean, let myself dry a bit in the breeze.

I had to smile, thinking of what a view some plane overhead would have had. I pulled my bottoms back up.

Later, the rain tapered off and the wind became a light breeze as the clouds finally broke. The sudden burst of warm sunshine spread over my exposed skin. My smile was automatic and genuine.

There were a few inches of water in the raft, which I was sick of sitting in. I wondered whether I should bail. Then I remembered the yellow cup and unzipped the Coastal Commander. Was it a bailer?

I stuck the cup into the water around me and scooped some up. Seemed like a bailer to me. After working for a while, I managed to reduce the water in the raft by quite a bit, so that the sun could actually dry most of it.

The Coastal Commander had redeemed itself slightly.

I wondered if Max would get sick, sitting in wet clothes with the head wound. I knew I couldn't sit in my wet clothes all day. Somehow

I needed to try to dry them. Max's too. Scooting over to him on my butt, I undid his tie, set it aside, and then unbuttoned his white shirt.

After that, I had to pause. How strange to be undressing him. Maybe I shouldn't. I mean, he probably wouldn't have done the same to me. Although that was different, wasn't it?

I shook my head to clear it, tried to take on the mental tone of a caregiver. I was just trying to help him, because he might really be injured. And might be worse off if he sat there in wet clothes. And I would feel terrible if I could do something, anything, and didn't. So I grabbed hold of his shirt and pulled it off him.

His T-shirt was thicker and wetter and harder to get off, but I pulled it over his head. His chest was tan and muscular, and something silver hung from a black cord around his neck.

"Max?

Max!"

He didn't answer.

I reached out and held it in my hand, then glanced up at his face. I hadn't really noticed before, but he was handsome. Even unshaven and asleep. I shook his shoulder a little. His eyes stayed closed and he didn't budge.

The silver at the end of the cord was oblong, with a swirly pattern of different blacks etched into the surface on one side. Something so familiar about it. Holding it in my hand, my glance rested on my thumb and I realized what the pattern was.

A thumbprint in the silver.

His own?

I pressed the silver thumbprint up against my own. They were very close in size.

Max's hands were considerably larger than mine, even though he wasn't that big a man. The print couldn't belong to him.

So whose was it?

A girlfriend's?

I wanted to know more, but he obviously wasn't talking at the moment. I let the thumbprint drop back against his chest.

A ragged scar ran down the length of his side. I wondered how he got it and whether he would tell me when he woke up. He seemed like the type to not want to tell stories about scars, like some people did.

He seemed like the type to not want to tell any stories at all.

I backed off with the clothes, tossing the T-shirt to a corner of the raft, then holding up the button-down so the wind could blow it around, drying the thin material fairly quickly. I put that back on him, which wasn't easy, but I felt a sense of satisfaction when I finished.

Then I took off my hoodie and tried the same drying trick. But the material was so thick that even after my arms got tired of holding the thing up, it wasn't near to being dry. I knew I should try to dry my camisole, since it was next to my skin.

I hesitated for a moment or two. Then, tired of being clammy, I turned my back to Max and pulled my camisole over my head, then held it up in the wind, trying not to think about the fact I was naked from the waist up in a raft with a man I didn't know.

My camisole was cotton and dried pretty quickly. The cloth felt so warm when I put it on, which made my wet Bermuda shorts feel even worse. I realized they would dry just as fast, if not faster, so, glancing at Max to make sure his eyes were still shut, I slipped those off as well. I told myself that having dry pants would be worth the few moments of embarrassment. And my pink underwear actually looked like—and covered more than—my bikini bottoms anyway, so it was all relative.

When my pants were dry and I put them back on, I turned around and asked him what had been on my mind for a while. "Do you think they're looking for us?"

No answer, as expected.

So I replied, "Of course they are."

Funny, it didn't make me feel any better.

I tried to think of something that would.

"People have survived for weeks in rafts. In way worse situations than this." One in particular came to mind.

Whenever we were down to no new DVDs to watch on Midway, I was forced to watch some older movies. One was about the USS *Indianapolis*, which, in 1945, was on a secret mission to the Mariana Islands to deliver components for the atom bomb that got dropped on Hiroshima a week later. The ship was on the way back to the Philippines when it got torpedoed by a Japanese submarine, and the massive ship went down in twelve minutes.

Strange, that the G-1 had almost taken longer to sink below the waves than a huge ship like that.

The survivors of the shipwreck were stuck out in the ocean with no lifeboats. Some were in life jackets, but some were only in what they had on. Some had jumped in the ocean wearing nothing but underwear.

And the mission was so secret that no one knew where they were, so no one knew they were missing. For four days and five nights, the crew, what was left of it, drifted in the ocean. A plane accidentally spotted the oil slick and the survivors were finally rescued. There were almost nine hundred to start, and only a little over three hundred survived the time in the water.

"See," I said out loud. "That was way worse."

But it was hard for me to think of anything worse than being in a raft in the middle of the ocean with no food or water, not knowing whether anyone would ever find us. Now that I had begun thinking about the movie, I couldn't stop.

Men dying from dehydration, going crazy. Sharks attacking.

A shudder ran through my body.

Living on Midway, I didn't like to think about sharks. But I was still fascinated by them.

Most people on the mainland seemed to think great white sharks were the worst, but I'd seen tiger sharks in action. Tiger sharks seemed to be killing machines, reacting only on instinct, which was to kill and eat, not necessarily in that order. They had the nickname "garbage can of the sea" because they'd eat anything. Including people. On Midway, women didn't even go in the water during their periods because the scent of blood might draw sharks. During albatross nesting season, when the young albatross were learning to fly off on their own, the waters around Midway attracted lots of tigers.

The young albatross touched down in the water when they got tired. Some of them didn't understand they had to fold in their wings, because once their wings got wet, they couldn't fly. So the stupid ones held their wings out as they sat in the water, but they weren't strong enough to keep them up for long, so of course they drooped until they touched the water and the feathers got wet.

Then the young birds couldn't take off.

And they were doomed.

The tiger sharks knew exactly when this would happen and, like clockwork, they showed up every late June, early July for their fill of albatross Happy Meals.

I'd been out in a boat with my dad one day when we saw a young albatross floating out in the lagoon. He started to motor toward it when all of a sudden a two-foot-wide gaping mouth shot up and devoured the bird in one bite, then disappeared below.

What scared me the most was that there was no warning, like in the movies, where you get the music and the fin in the water and then the strike. In reality, with the tigers, there was simply a dark shape in the water, a glimpse of that shadow, shiny gray skin, and then instant death.

So I had no time for people talking about great whites. Tigers are the true monsters of the sea. And I did not relish having a mere inch or so of inflated rubber between me and them.

I shut my eyes and tried to sleep.

No such luck.

# seventeen

By that evening, with the help of the sun and the warm breeze, I felt a little drier, except that my clothes were stiff from the salt water. But it beat sitting there in wet ones all night. I had to accept we weren't getting rescued that day. My skin stung from all the salt that had dried on it. I tried to think about other things. It would help if I had someone to talk to.

But Max was still sleeping.

I wanted him to wake up. I felt alone again, too alone.

"Max?"

He didn't move.

"Max. Max!"

Nothing.

Sliding over to him, I grabbed his arm, shaking it a bit. He didn't stir.

"Max." I actually slapped his cheek lightly, and then laid my hand against it. His warm skin was sandpapery with whiskers and I let my hand linger there a moment as I said his name again, and slid my trembling fingers down and around his neck until I felt his pulse.

I breathed out and leaned back.

I was tired too, and I hadn't even hit my head. I'd read that sometimes your body knew when you needed rest and kept you asleep.

Well, actually, that was more like a coma. But I didn't think Max was in a coma.

I hoped not anyway.

Folding up my hoodie, I placed it on his lap, and laid my head down, hoping he wouldn't mind. The position was comfortable . . . almost comforting.

I closed my eyes.

My stomach growled, so empty it almost hurt. My throat was dry when I swallowed, but I tried to push the discomfort away. Finally the rhythm of the waves, gentle and calm, put me to sleep.

I awoke to a sliver of moon and a multitude of stars overhead, and a warm breeze. Still hungry and thirsty, I also noticed another discomfort: My shorts were cool and damp again. Was the raft leaking?

## eighteen

My hands almost completely submerged in the cool water as I felt around the bottom of the raft. There was at least an inch of water, maybe more. But it didn't seem to be getting wetter.

Had I been asleep that long?

Maybe it had rained.

But my shirt was still dry. I felt around until I found the bailer, and then scooped until I could barely feel any water in the bottom.

"Max?"

He didn't answer. Quickly I laid my fingers on his neck, found his pulse. Was it fainter than before?

I didn't think he was supposed to sleep that long if he had a concussion. I needed to wake him up.

With both hands on his shoulders, I shook him. "Max!" He didn't stir. "Wake up! Come on."

I felt again for a pulse.

Faint. Oh so faint.

Curling myself up, I laid my head down in his lap, my eyes scrunched, and, even though I was parched and famished, tried to sleep.

The sun woke me up, bright and hot, with not a cloud in sight.

I licked my lips. They were so dry, they burned.

Only then did I realize our new enemy.

We were already thirsty, but the sun and heat would only make us more so. Hunger sucked too, but people lasted a lot longer without food than they did without water. I tried to remember the movie about the *Indianapolis* survivors, how long they had lasted without water.

I tried to tell myself they had it way worse than we did.

We had a raft.

They had been stuck in only life vests, floating defenseless in the ocean. I would not have lasted even a day like that. I would have lost my mind imagining what was there beneath me as I floated.

But then, they had also had each other.

I glanced over at Max. Even unconscious, he was still there. I could do this, as long as I wasn't alone.

I reached forward to check his pulse again, but then my hand froze in midair, stopping before it reached his neck.

There was no reason to check his pulse.

Max was fine. Completely fine. He was just asleep.

He'd been through a lot and he'd been injured and he needed to sleep. And I was going to let him. Almost by itself, my hand reached out and rested on his neck. Was that a pulse? Yes. Yes, I felt it. A very faint drumming, but it was there. *It was.*

He'd fallen over a little, and something poked out from behind him. I pulled on it. His ditty bag. I'd forgotten about it ever since he'd shoved it behind him. I held it in my lap for a moment, then squeezed, feeling the shapes inside. Beneath my touch plastic rustled, and something felt like a book. Almost involuntarily, my hands caressed the bag for a moment.

I glanced at Max, then back to the bag.

No, I wasn't opening it.

The bag belonged to him. He'd have to open it. Besides, he would probably be pretty pissed when he woke up and saw I'd gone through it, so I pushed it back behind him, where I'd found it.

There was more water in the bottom of the raft again, and I bailed, trying to keep us dry. I wanted Max to wake up, to talk to me, to talk to me about anything. I didn't care what. Even sharks would have been an acceptable topic at that point.

"Did you know sharks are the only fish that blink with both eyes?"

No response, as expected.

I sighed. Was it too much to want someone to talk to?

# nineteen

After a few hours of intermittent bailing, I realized there was definitely a leak somewhere that was not going to stop letting water in. Something had to be done about it.

Without thinking, I checked Max's neck again. My fingertips couldn't find a heartbeat and my own speeded up. I set my head against his chest, listening. Was that a heartbeat?

Of course, of course it was.

I sat up. *Max is fine. He's young and strong and he's just resting.*

"But there's barely a heartbeat." I said it aloud. Did that make it true, me saying it aloud? No. "No one dies from a bump on the head." Do they?

Again, I checked for a pulse, then listened with my head on his chest. His chest was warm, not cold. He would be cold if he was dead, right?

My face turned up to the sky and the sun. The day was hot. Even a dead cold fish would be warm after sitting out on a day like that.

*Stop it!*

My head sunk into my hands.

What was I supposed to do? Someone needed to tell me what to do.

"Tell me what to do!" I screamed at the sky. "Tell me what to do!" I sobbed. "Tell me what to do."

My dry throat hurt enough even without the yelling, so I stopped.

Meanwhile, the raft continued to leak water and I knew I was losing the strength to bail.

If we, me and Max, continued as we were, the raft would founder and we would end up in the ocean. Our combined weight, my 115, his probably 165, 170, was too much.

Would there be a difference with only my weight in the raft? Would it stop taking on water and stay afloat?

We had to stay afloat, stay in the raft. The alternative was not worth thinking about. No. Worse than that. The alternative was unbearable. I would not survive if I had to float in the water.

Once more, I laid my head on his chest. I held his hand, which was definitely not warm. I rubbed it, trying to help get the circulation back, telling myself that's why it seemed stiff. "No." I turned my face into his chest. He smelled salty, like the ocean, with just a hint of cologne of some sort. "You're going to be fine. I can't be alone."

I stayed that way for so long that there was time for several inches of water to gather in the raft, making me so far behind in the bailing that catching up might not be possible. My options seemed to be steering toward one, the one I dreaded the most.

## twenty

Holding Max's hands, I leaned back, pulling him forward. He barely budged, and I knew that wouldn't work. So I let go and he fell back where he'd been.

The life vest he'd worn off the plane still sat in the corner. Kneeling in front of him, I struggled to put the vest on him.

My voice was as calm and soothing as I could make it. "It will just be for a while, until I can get the raft bailed. I won't leave you. I promise."

Rolling him onto his side, I got close behind him and pushed. The bottom was slippery, so he slid easily over to edge. Using all my strength, I managed to get Max's left arm and leg over the side.

He was half in, half out, sprawled like a bug on the side of the raft. My vision was blurry. Was I crying? "I'm sorry."

My plan was to roll him the rest of the way over, so he would be faceup in the water. Just until I could empty the raft. A few minutes, at most. If I saw a shark, I'd get him back inside. Somehow.

There was a nylon line on the raft and I tied that to his life vest. "I won't let you go. I promise."

He didn't wake up. And he didn't hear my promise.

With less weight in the raft, and bailing like crazy, I managed to catch up. There didn't seem to be any new water coming in, which brightened my mood.

Then I looked over at Max's bag. Yellow and round, like a fat cylinder, it had a rolled top with a black plastic buckle.

What if there was something in it that could help us?

But if there was, he would have used it that first night.

Wouldn't he?

But then, as I thought about it, what could have possibly been in there that could help us?

Maybe food. A cell phone. Something . . .

Reaching out, I held the bag for a moment, considering.

The bag was private property. It belonged to Max. Opening it without his permission would be wrong. I undid the buckle, and then told myself I should put it back.

Instead, I unrolled the top and pulled the zipper.

## twenty-one

Slowly, I unfolded a sheaf of papers. Before I started reading, I smoothed the creases with my hand. The top page was the manifest for our flight. Larry was listed on top, then Max, then the cargo. I flipped through the pages, not sure what I was looking for. Something nagged at me as I scanned the pages, and then it hit me.

*Where was my name?*

My name might not have been typed, like the rest. There hadn't been time, so it might be in handwriting. I flipped through the pages again, looking for handwritten items. Looking for the words *Robie Mitchell*.

But other than signatures, Larry's and the guy in charge of loading's, there wasn't anything handwritten anywhere.

Again, I flipped. I scanned. I pored over every page until my eyes blurred. But I still couldn't find my name.

I ran through that night of the flight, trying to recall every detail.

I'd fallen asleep in the lounge. Larry had come and gotten me. He'd asked me something.

*What?*

My breaths shallowed and quickened as I tried to remember. The papers shook in my hands.

He'd asked something about paperwork. Had he mentioned Max? I thought I remembered Larry saying his name.

Was Max supposed to do my paperwork and he forgot?

My breath caught in my throat.

There was one thing I knew for sure.

I had never stepped on a scale that evening. Which meant I had never gotten weighed and neither had my bags.

I let the papers fall into my lap as I covered my face with both hands.

My weight, plus the weight of my bags, were all pounds over what the G-1 could carry with one engine. I should have said something. I had never stepped foot on that plane before without getting weighed, even when we flew in a relatively empty plane from Midway to Honolulu.

But I had been groggy from sleeping . . . anxious to go home . . . worried about the flight . . .

I dropped my hands and stared out at the horizon.

Had my extra weight, and the weight of my bags, brought us down?

What did I know for sure?

Basically, that my 115 pounds never got recorded. And neither did my bags, and they were stuffed, probably close to 75 pounds in total. Which added up to almost 200 pounds too heavy for the one remaining engine.

Grabbing the papers again, I looked for my name. They could have estimated, right? Maybe they didn't list my name; maybe they just added the estimated weight of me and my bags to cargo. Or maybe they had taken off something that weighed the same as me and my bags, but not written it down.

Larry had written my weight down for other flights, he might have known what to estimate, even added a few pounds for a cushion, just to be sure.

I nodded.

*Absolutely.* That made much more sense. Larry was too smart to make a mistake like that.

Feeling better, I thought of another scenario. They could have weighed my bags when I was asleep, then brought them back, I wouldn't have even known.

That had to be it.

They flew so much, they would never make a mistake like that.

Still, even if my weight was on there, even if it hadn't been too much for the one engine, there was one other thing, one thing that might be the worst fact of all. And for all my rationalizing, I couldn't explain it away.

*My name was not on the manifest.*

## twenty-two

If my name was not on the list, then nobody knew I was on that flight. Except Larry and Max.

But Larry was gone.

And Max was with me.

The flight manager, the bald guy filling in that night, he knew, *right*?

I breathed out and set the papers on my lap.

But that night had been crazy, people running around. He didn't know me, had only sent me to Larry, and had not actually given me the go-ahead. When I talked to him, I didn't even have my bags with me. All I'd asked him was where Suzanne was. For all he knew, I was just there to see her, not to get on the plane.

And all the loaders had already left when I got on the plane. It was dark. No one saw me get on except for Larry and Max.

I folded the papers, unable to look at them anymore, and shoved them back in the bag.

Next I found a laminated card. Labeled "Survival at Sea," it was a list of items, in addition to a bunch of small type.

On top of the list was the heading REMEMBER!

I couldn't help but picture some grandma lady admonishing me with a raised finger. *Robie, now remember:*

1. **Do not drink seawater.**

   Whoops. I imagine I'd had a few gallons that first night, when I fell in the water.

2. **Do not drink urine.**

   Wasn't planning to.

3. **Do not drink alcohol.**

4. **Do not smoke.**

   Those two were just stupid and I breathed out a half-hearted "duh."

5. **Do not eat, unless water is available.**

   That didn't make much sense. If food presented itself, believe me, I was going to eat it.

The next item on the card said the two biggest causes of death in shipwrecks were drowning—

*Um, been there, almost done that.*

And hypothermia.

I hoped it was a warm enough time of year to avoid that. I hadn't been chilled since the first night and day. Plus, I figured that was a bigger danger if you didn't have a raft and had to be in the water the whole time. Which, as I kept reading, it seemed being in an inflatable raft, as I was, was actually the best way to survive at sea.

Good to know that I was doing *something* right.

The other things on the card weren't all applicable. One was about getting away from a sinking ship because it could suck you down. Another was about an oil slick from a plane or ship, because it could light up. There was a whole paragraph about swimming underwater to escape the fire.

Well, that was one problem I hadn't had. Thank God for small favors. My plane crashed, but at least there wasn't a fiery oil slick to deal with.

I kept reading, and the next section was about dehydration.

**In order to reduce loss of water through sweat, soak your clothes in the sea and wring them out.**
I groaned. All that time wasted trying to get my clothes dry.

**But be aware that too much of this method of cooling can result in saltwater boils and rashes.**
What was a saltwater boil? I didn't really want to find out.

**Be careful not to get the bottom of the raft wet.**
The raft had never been dry.

**In arctic waters, old sea ice may be used for water.**
I sighed. There weren't exactly any glaciers floating around me.

**You may get water from fish. Drink the aqueous fluid found along the spine and in the eyes of large fish.**
"Ew." I would have to be really desperate for that to happen, that's for sure.

**Watch the clouds, and be ready for any chance of rain. Keep the tarpaulin ready for catching water.**

"That might be nice if I HAD A STUPID TARPAULIN!"

Apparently, the Survival at Sea people assumed you would be equipped with things needed in order to survive at sea.

*Idiots.*

I shoved the card back in the ditty bag without reading any more.

Looking further, I found a red single-subject spiral notebook, curved to the shape of the ditty bag. I glanced at the words on the cover, frowned, and fanned the pages. They were full of handwriting, but it was definitely an invasion of privacy. If Max wanted me to know what was in there, he would tell me. I glanced down at him, his face still serene.

Still, I put the notebook back without reading any of it. Inside the ditty bag was one more thing, something red. I reached in and pulled it out.

I whooped when I saw what it was.

# twenty-three

Despite my major thirst, my mouth began watering immediately.

A king-size bag of Skittles.

My gaze went to Max.

I swallowed.

Would he share when he woke up? He didn't owe me anything. He'd already saved my life.

He could have told me the first night. "Hey, we're adrift at sea, but I have Skittles."

*Taste the rainbow.*

My heart beat faster as I licked my lips.

*Taste the rainbow.*

He'd had plenty of time to tell me about them.

*Taste the rainbow.*

The truth was, he had been hiding the only food on the raft from me.

*Taste the rainbow.*

"Screw you, Max." Carefully spreading my sweatshirt in my lap, I gently tore open the bag of Skittles and shook them out onto my shirt.

At first, I could only stare as my heart pounded.

Then I counted them.

One hundred and seven all together.

Sorting them into piles by color with a trembling hand, I counted again.

Thirteen red.

Twenty-three yellow.

Twenty-two orange.

Thirty-two green.

Seventeen purple.

I didn't like purple Skittles. They tasted like really bad grape juice. Max could have all of those. I would fight him for the green and the orange though. They were my favorites.

There was one deformed orange Skittle.

I didn't think Max would mind whether I ate the bad one.

Did I even care what Max did or didn't mind?

My hesitation was momentary before I popped it in my mouth and sucked, trying to make the fruitiness last as long as possible. The rest I put back in the Skittles bag, one by one, then put that into the ditty bag and zipped it up before replacing it.

*Dumb.*

He'd know as soon as he saw the Skittles bag that I'd been in his stuff.

But I didn't really care. My mouth still tasted of orange candy. I opened my hand. My fingers, still wet and wrinkled, had the colors of the rainbow all over them. I licked my palm, then, one at a time, I stuck my fingers in my mouth and sucked, savoring. And getting rid of the evidence.

My butt was wet. Time to bail again.

## twenty-four

I managed to clear just about all the water out of the raft. Probably not dry enough for the Survival at Sea people, but, hey, it was the best I could do.

The sun beat down, and I put the damp hoodie on top of my head to keep the hot rays off my face. Max's face was uncovered, so I took his T-shirt, sopped from lying in the wet bottom of the raft, and draped it over him. Hopefully it wouldn't result in any saltwater boils.

I shut my eyes and, before I knew it, was waking up. My throat was dry and my stomach still rumbled. The sun was still up, but lower in the sky and, once again, I was sitting in water.

I leaned over to check on Max.

He was gone.

"Max!"

Shading my eyes, I scanned the ocean around the raft. "Max!"

*Oh my God, what have I done?*

"Max!" I screamed his name until I was hoarse and the water in the raft had gotten too deep to ignore any longer. I started some frantic bailing as I kept calling for Max and my thoughts raced.

"Max!"

*He's in the life jacket, he won't sink. He'll be okay.*

"Max!"

*He'll wake up and come after me.*

"Max!"

*The current will bring him the same way.*

*Won't it?*

*Wouldn't he be here if that were true?*

I shook the thoughts away so I could concentrate on the bailing. Then I could focus on getting Max back.

Soon, it became clear that my efforts were not going to be enough. I was not going to be able to bail enough to empty out the raft. The best thing would be to get out, flip the raft and empty the water, then get back in.

There wasn't another life jacket, which meant I would have to stay afloat by hanging on to the raft. Steeling myself, I put one foot over the side and into the water.

And froze.

There was no way. I could not get in that water.

I pulled my foot back in and sat down. The water in the raft continued to rise beneath me. I knew there was no choice, so I stuck my foot over the side again. This time, it stayed for a few minutes before I pulled it back in.

No way was I getting out of that raft on my own.

I would stay there until it sank beneath the waves, taking me with it for good. I needed something to make me feel better, something to make me feel like I wasn't stuck in a raft by myself in the middle of the godforsaken ocean.

Grabbing Max's bag, I unzipped it, snatching out the bag of Skittles. Shaking some into my palm, I slammed them into my mouth, chewing, tasting every flavor, not even minding the grape. As soon as I swallowed those, I downed another handful before noticing the bag was half empty.

My mouth dropped open. "Oh my God."

What was I doing? The candy belonged to Max.

And for the time being, at least, it was our only food.

Was I already going crazy from the sun and the thirst? Was this how long it had taken the survivors of the *Indianapolis* to lose it?

*Get a grip, Robie. Get a grip.*

I shoved the Skittles back in the ditty bag and tossed it to the other side of the raft.

My chin quivered and my lips curled as a guttural wail escaped between them.

Sobs bubbled up, great gulping, gasping sobs that racked my whole body, complete with tears that blurred my vision so that my whole reality was messed up. And so I screamed, shouting at the sky, "I don't want to be here! I don't want to be here!"

*I want to be anywhere but here.*

## twenty-five

No longer in the raft, no longer fifteen, no longer in command of my world, I was but five. A little kid of five and I'd awoken from a heinous nightmare and wanted my mother, wanted her to take away everything that was bad.

With a fist on either side of my face, I scrunched my eyes shut. "Mommy! Where are you? Where are you?"

Rocking back and forth, I struggled to get the words out amidst the sobs and the gasps and the shudders.

"Mommy! I want you!" I wanted her to answer me. "I need you!"

"Just come and get me!" I said it over and over, until the words turned quiet, a desperate pleading. "Just come and get me. Please. Mommy. Please."

My voice cracked on the last "Come and get me . . . Mommy . . ."

And then I could only think it.

*Mommy. Please come get me.*

But she didn't.

*Someone please tell me something worse.*

And that's when I knew no one could tell me something worse. Because there wasn't anything.

I was still alone. In a raft. At sea.

## twenty-six

Me. It was all on me. Everything was all on me.

As much as I hoped for it, my mom was not coming to get me. I was the only help I was getting. And I needed to chill out before I lost it completely.

The Skittles rose in my throat and I swallowed, forcing them to stay down. No way was I throwing up food, the only food there was.

*Get a grip. I have to get a grip. Think, Robie. You can do this. Do what you need to do to make it through this. Do what you need to do.*

I considered what I needed to do.

*You have only yourself to rely on. But you know a lot. A lot. You live on an island, which is basically just a bigger raft that doesn't move. You've picked up so much information. You know enough to survive this, you know you do.*

*You, on your own, are strong enough to survive.*

I took a deep breath, which held just a trace of lingering shudder, and let it out.

I would do this. I would be my own resource. I would get through this whichever way I could.

Starting immediately, I would do what was necessary to stay hopeful.

To believe I would survive.

Something grabbed my hand and I screamed.

# twenty-seven

"It's me." Max let go and I turned toward him.

"You're back!" I almost told him I thought he was gone forever, but didn't see what good that would do. Especially when he looked worse than death. A sense of relief rushed over me.

"How long have I been out?" He held a hand to his head.

That was an easy answer. "A long time."

The line was gone. So was his life jacket.

He held on to the raft and pulled himself upright. He stuck a hand in the raft. "It's really leaking."

I nodded, feeling so guilty. "I'm so sorry I put you in the water. I just thought . . ."

"You weigh less. Together, we'd sink."

"Yeah." I thought for sure he'd be pissed about being in the water, and was glad that he agreed it was the smart thing to do. I was glad he was back, calm and rational, just in time, just when I was in danger of losing it.

He said, "We need to fix it."

I knew that, I did. "How?"

He pointed to a pocket in the raft. "There should be a patch kit in there. But we need to empty the raft first. Then find the leak."

I felt in the pocket and pulled out a small pouch. Inside I found a little tube of sealant, some small patches of the same rubber as the raft, and a small sheet of instructions. Scanning them, I figured out what I needed to do.

"We need to tie those down," Max said, pointing to the Coastal Commander and the bailer. Then he pointed at his ditty bag. "Put that around your wrist."

I just sat there. It was his bag. If something happened, if, heaven forbid, we got split up, it was his bag. It should stay with him.

He said, "Do it."

Taking his bag, I slipped the bungee cord around my wrist.

I knew what he'd say next, but my heart still sunk when I heard the words.

"Now you need to get out."

I didn't answer.

"I'm right here. I won't let anything happen. You need to get out so we can flip this over and fix it."

Taking a deep breath, I put my foot over the side and started to slide out of the raft and into the water. But then I locked my elbows on the edge, refusing to go farther. My weight on the side of the empty raft made it flip over, trapping me underneath.

I screamed and grabbed for the raft, pushing it up. "Get it off! Get it off!" Even though, for the moment, I could breathe just fine within the pocket of air between me and the capsized raft, the feeling of my legs just hanging there, treading, was more than I could take. "Get it off me!" I screamed. I couldn't stand it anymore and didn't wait for Max. Instead, I shoved up with all my strength, throwing the raft off me.

As I did, the ditty bag attached to my arm slipped off. I grabbed for it, catching it by the bottom. Red and green and purple and yellow and orange dots rained down around me, some pelting me.

Skittles.

"No!" I scrambled, splashing as I tried to grab them, but they were everywhere, sinking. How could I have forgotten to close the bag?

In a frenzy, I scooped water and managed to get a few. Two yellow, a green, and a purple. I dropped them back in the ditty bag and searched for more.

Nothing.

They had sunk.

Holding on to the raft with one hand, slapping at the water with the other, I blubbered, as part of me cursed the carelessness that had just lost us all the food we had, and another part was just pissed that I hadn't eaten them all when I had the chance.

Sniffling, I wiped my nose, nearly jumping out of my skin at the sudden streak of pain. Touching it again, gently, my piercing was hot to the touch and hurt like hell. Great.

Max said nothing. Nothing about the bag or the Skittles. Instead, he stated exactly what I was thinking, the one thing that mattered so much more than the stupid candy. "I hope the patch kit is still in there."

## twenty-eight

Inhaling a shudder, I looked inside the ditty bag, hoping to hell I hadn't lost the patch kit. I sighed with relief when I saw it.

I knew I needed to patch the raft. My hands shook as I fought a rising panic, trying not to think about what might be in the water. Anything could sneak up on me.

Hurt me.

Eat me.

I'd read that many victims of shark attacks didn't even feel the actual bite. They just had the sensation of something bumping them. Only after they got out of the water, if they survived, did they see the holes in their wetsuits, and the bite marks on their skin.

Because most sharks took a bite of humans and didn't much care for the taste.

Most sharks.

Tigers didn't give a crap. Food was food.

I squinted and looked around me. The surface of the ocean was blue, a shiny mirror reflecting the sun.

I wasn't exactly sure how to find the leak. I thought maybe if I pushed the raft up partway, slid under it, and dripped down water from the bailer, then I could see where water came through.

I pulled myself up on one side of the upside-down raft, forcing the other side to tip up. I took the bailer and filled it, then tossed the water up on the back side as I watched underneath for any water dripping. The first ten times, I saw nothing. And I was getting too tired to keep doing it. Then, finally I saw a drip. I quickly filled the bailer again, aiming for the same area. And water came through.

"Max! I found it!"

Once I'd seen the pinprick hole, it appeared so obvious I wondered how I'd missed it before. I got out from under the raft and clambered partway up the bottom of the raft and found the leak. Carefully, I squeezed out some of the glue stuff and stuck the patch on.

"Nice job," said Max.

Then I slipped back into the water and bobbed there, trying not to lose my mind.

There was an emergency valve, and I blew into that until the raft seemed completely inflated.

I wanted to crawl back inside so bad. Wet and shivering, I wanted out of the water. But Max made me wait a little more, just to be sure the patch held.

"Okay," he said finally.

I had to shove the raft back over, so I held both hands on one edge. "One . . . two . . . three!" I grunted and shoved. The raft went up on its edge and started to flip, just as a gust of wind caught hold, rolling the raft end over end, like a coin on a floor, away from me.

"Noooooooooooooooooooooo!"

We watched helplessly as the raft finally came to a stop, right side up, about fifty yards away.

Max wasn't strong enough.

I would have to swim for it.

## twenty-nine

On my stomach, I started to stroke with my arms as I kicked. But I didn't like the water coming up in my face, and the ditty bag on my arm hampered my progress. So I flipped over on my back.

Even as a kid, I had done okay on my back.

I breathed out. That was better. Much better. I didn't feel like anything was dangling.

But I also couldn't see where I was going, could only guess. I pulled with my arms and kicked for a count of ten, then stopped to turn and see where the raft was.

After doing that three or four times, I realized I wasn't even gaining on the raft. I might even be losing. So I did the dog paddle, which seemed even slower than my backstroke had been.

Max was close behind me and called out, "You need to swim on your stomach. Just aim for the raft, hold your breath, and go."

I didn't want to.

Then he asked exactly what I'd been asking myself: "Do you want to be stuck out here, without the raft?"

No.

I took the ditty bag off my wrist and put the bungee cord around my neck, setting the ditty bag on my back. It was very tight, almost constricting, but at least it would stay put while I swam.

Turning back on my stomach, I took a deep breath, put my head in the water, and did a pathetic front crawl as fast and far as I could until I had to breathe. Then I paused, floated for a bit, just to the edge of panic, and then went again.

I swore *if*, no, *when* I got out of this, I would learn to swim properly. How stupid, to not know how to swim. *Everyone* knew how to swim.

I paused, floated again. Did the raft seem closer?

No. With no weight in it, the raft was cruising along, much faster than I was. If I didn't hurry, it would be out of reach before I knew it.

I adjusted the ditty bag, held my breath, and stuck my face in the water.

My arms and legs were strong, I could do the strokes. But rhythmic breathing. I could never get the rhythmic breathing part. I'd tried and tried, through swim lesson after swim lesson.

I stopped again and bobbed, too weary to be panicked at the dangling of my limbs.

My breaths were deep and ragged, and my arms and legs burned. The raft was about twenty yards off, so I had gained.

But I had to keep going.

I had to make it to the raft. I had to make it. I had to.

*Had to.*

I sucked in a breath and went, pulling as hard as I could with my arms as my legs kicked until they threatened to fall off. My breath was used up, it was time to surface. I stuck my head up, tried to swim that way, but it didn't work. Still, I kept stroking and kicking, as I took another breath and stuck my head in again.

*Make it make it make it make it*

My lungs were ready to burst but I kept going, my arms and legs burning, until I couldn't do it anymore. I hoped the raft was there, hoped it was within reach. Because I couldn't swim anymore.

I was spent.

I stopped, lifting my head to suck in sweet air. I hoped the raft was there, where it had to be. *Was it there?*

I opened my eyes to see.

## thirty

The raft was there, only a few yards away. I flipped to my back and kicked the rest of the way until my head bumped into it. I turned over and held on to the side until I caught my breath. I pulled the ditty bag from around my neck and dropped it into the raft. Then I tried to pull myself in, but my arms were too tired.

So I tried putting one leg over the side.

No luck.

No way was I staying in that water.

I put both my elbows up on the raft and pulled until my chin was there. Then, grunting, I heaved one leg up on the side. I wasn't there yet, but I wasn't going to lose the progress I'd made, so I lay there awhile, panting, waiting for my strength to come back.

At last, with a final burst, I pulled myself up and over, and I slid face-first into the raft, where I just lay, recovering. Then I remembered the whole goal of my ordeal. The patch.

Was anything wet?

Other than the water the raft had picked up in its tumble across the waves, there didn't seem to be any more. As far as I could tell, there were no leaks. Realizing I'd been holding my breath, I let it out.

"One issue solved."

I sat up. Max was already in the raft and sat opposite of me, where he leaned his head back and closed his eyes.

I hoped the patch job was enough to hold both of us.

Wiped out, I rolled over on my back and glanced up at the sky. There wasn't a cloud anywhere. No rain meant no drinking water. My throat was so dry. And then I remembered my nose. Wincing as I touched the diamond stud with my fingertips, I twisted it slightly and nearly passed out from the pain. My eyes watered and I squeezed them shut, moaning as I tried to stay still, tried to will the pain away. I took deep breaths, like my mom had taught me when I was eight and broke my arm.

I hadn't put alcohol on the piercing since before leaving AJ's. Probably close to forty-eight hours. Could it already be infected?

Max wasn't watching, and still sat there with his eyes closed.

I filled the yellow bailer with salt water, held my breath, and stuck my nose in it. It stung. And while I wasn't sure, it seemed like salt water might help. Even though the guy had told me to stay away from the ocean, my mom made me gargle with salt water when I had a sore throat, so it seemed like there had to be something healing about it. I took a breath and dunked my nose back in a couple more times.

It seemed like weeks had passed since that day I'd gotten my nose pierced. How long had it really been? Two or three days?

I sighed.

I had been a different person, just thinking about stupid stuff like diamonds in my nose. Set on doing something my parents didn't want me to do, simply because I could.

*My parents.*

I wanted to be with them, even if they didn't always let me do what I wanted. I didn't care. I would never care again if I could only get back to them.

My muscles still burned and I laid my head on the cushy edge of the raft, to rest for a moment, and shut my eyes. "I'm just resting for a little while, okay, Max?"

When I awoke, the sun was still high in the sky. My face was on fire, and I had a pounding headache. My thirst was becoming unbearable.

I pinched a piece of skin on the back of my hand and let go. The skin stayed up, in a little mound, before slowly going back.

*Sick.*

Normally, if you pinch the skin on your hand like that, it springs back immediately. But when you're dehydrated it'll stay up, take longer to bounce back.

I pinched the back of Max's hand. I had to turn away when I saw his skin took longer to settle than mine had. So much longer.

Although, maybe he was always like that. I had no way of knowing.

I was stuck on a raft with a person I knew hardly anything about. I wondered if being there with someone I knew would have been easier. But there were plenty of adults I knew that I most definitely would not want to be stuck on a raft with.

I had my own theories about adults. Mostly, they fell into two categories. The first, the ones I called the Regurgitators, think you want to know everything about them. Even when they ask you a question, like "So what do you like to do?" they still find a way to turn it around and make it about themselves.

The second are the Hoovers, they keep asking and asking and asking about you, sucking you dry of every bit of your life story.

Of course, some adults ask and tell equally.

"Max, where are you from?" I waited a moment, but he didn't answer.

And then there are people like Max. I put him in the couldn't-give-a-crap category. I knew he was injured and maybe sick, but still . . .

Max didn't seem shy. He didn't seem to care what I was doing on the plane without my parents, why I lived out in Midway, none of that.

Maybe I was being mean, since he did save my life. But I was stuck in a raft with him. And I was beginning to think he might be the last person I ever talked to.

There were a few things I could figure out on my own. He was a pilot. He was definitely new in the G-1 job, and he probably just got his pilot's license in the last few years. And he had to go to some kind of aviation school to do that, so he must be smart. Pilots had to know math and physics and other difficult subjects.

He probably had a girlfriend. No ring, so no wife. Although he could have lost it or maybe just didn't wear it. Or he could be divorced. There really wasn't any way to tell much at all. Which brought me back to the silver thumbprint. It had to belong to a girl. A girl that meant enough to Max that he wore her print around his neck.

My eyes went to the ditty bag and that spiral notebook with handwriting in it. A journal? Max didn't seem like the journaling type.

Just as I was seriously thinking about invading his privacy, he moved. "That's mine," he said.

"I know, sorry." I didn't want to hand him the bag. If he hadn't seen me freaking out in the water over the Skittles, he'd only have to look in the bag to see they were gone and then he'd know what I'd done. So I put it back in the corner of the raft.

"It's my journal."

"I didn't read it." It was the truth; I couldn't feel guilty about that.

"What do you want to know?"

Was he going to open up and actually talk about himself? I shrugged. "I'm not nosy, I just . . . I mean, we're stuck here, together, and it's weird I don't know anything about you really. Like where you're from."

He shrugged. "I don't like to talk about where I'm from. People have a way of making you feel stupid when you aren't from somewhere they've heard of. Like being from a city everyone knows about makes you better than other people."

I nodded. "Sometimes I feel that way too. No one has even been to where I'm from."

"I'm not from anywhere that anyone has ever heard of. I grew up on a ranch in the high desert of eastern Oregon, middle of flippin' nowhere. Nearest Walmart was two hours away."

I rolled my eyes. "I've got that beat. On Midway, my nearest Walmart is thousands of miles away."

"Our town was okay. Not much there, that's for sure. A Mc-Donald's. A farm and ranch store. Subway. Rite-Aid. An old movie theater. But the screen was dark and the sound sucked."

I smiled. "We have an old theater on Midway." My nose wrinkled. "It smells musty. There's a DVD player rigged up so we can play movies on the big screen. Once I was in there by myself, watching an old World War II movie. All of a sudden, I felt like the theater was full, full of people. I turned around to see, but there was still only me."

Max went on. "At school, sports were pretty big, but I wasn't, so I wrestled. Even though my natural weight was closer to a hundred thirty, I wrestled one twelve because seniors had the other slots all sewed up." He paused. "That whole season, I was hungry. Starving."

My stomach rumbled. I knew how he felt.

"Every night when I got home, dinner was a banana and fifty push-ups."

I shook my head. "That sounds barbaric." But the thought of a banana was almost heavenly.

"Not getting to drink as much water as I wanted was almost worse."

As dry as my throat was, I had to agree with that.

"But the absolute worst was Christmas. I didn't get to eat any of Ma's cookies. She made fudge, divinity, caramel pretzels, cookies with chunks of Snickers in them, some with Rolos. Spritz. My favorites were the frosted snowmen sugar cookies."

I licked my parched lips. I wanted one of those snowmen. So *bad*.

He continued. "Once, the night before a tournament, I went down to the kitchen after everyone was asleep. I told myself I was just going to get a glass of water. But instead, I went into the pantry where all the cookies were. I thought, just one. One Spritz wreath. A hundred fifty calories. I could run those off in a half hour. But it was so good, I ate another. A blue diamond. Another, a green cross . . . then the snowmen . . . the snickerdoodles." He stopped for a moment. "Peanut-butter cookies with the chocolate kiss in the middle."

"I make those with my mom." I teared up a little.

"How many calories? Ten thousand? And I had to make one twelve in less than eight hours. I started to sweat, maybe from all the sugar . . . maybe from panic. There was only one thing to do: I went over to the backdoor and stepped into my work boots without tying the laces. Got a jacket on and scuffed outside to the nearest snowbank. Snow was falling, and the flakes sparkled in the moonlight. I admired the night for a moment. Then, I stuck my finger down my throat."

I didn't know what to say, so I didn't say anything.

"It was dumb, eating all those cookies. I was just so hungry."

I knew the feeling.

## thirty-one

Max was still, his eyes closed again.

How strange, to learn so much about him all at once. Though I still didn't know who the thumbprint belonged to. I wanted to ask, but I got the feeling it wasn't any of my business. I would only learn what he wanted to tell me, and that had to be enough.

For now.

Once more, the sun was low in the sky. Our second full day at sea was almost over. If anyone had ever asked how long I thought I could survive in a raft on the sea, I'd have said I couldn't do it at all. Nothing in my life had ever prepared me for something like that. It wasn't like my home-school curriculum included Survival at Sea.

Still, I was coming up on forty-eight hours of survival. Which made me feel . . .

Nothing.

No, that wasn't right. I felt something.

Numb. Blurred. Fuzzy.

Dulled.

Like none of it was real. Except for the hunger pangs in my stomach.

I'd never been without food or water this long. Once in a while

I'd gone without lunch or something, but there's a big difference between missing lunch and not knowing if you'll eat again.

I was thirsty and ravenously hungry, especially after hearing about
the cookies. My nose had started throbbing. I didn't even try to touch
it. Thinking about the last time was enough to make me shudder as I
relived the fireball of pain that had shot into my head.

I reached into the ditty bag and dug out the few remaining Skittles
I'd managed to save. Their colors had bled, and some were half white,
while some were an ugly orangey brown.

REMEMBER! **5. Do not eat, unless water is available.**

Ignoring the Survival at Sea wisdom, I popped the candy into
my mouth, chewing, trying not to think about Max and how angry
he'd be.

But Max appeared well past the point of caring about Skittles. He
was so still, he seemed unconscious from the effort of talking.

The stars came out in the dusk sky. The moon rose, again just a
sliver, but it would provide enough light for me to see. If it hadn't
been for the hunger and thirst and, well, being stuck in a raft, I might
have thought it was a beautiful night.

Maybe my parents were looking up at the sky too. Worrying
about me. AJ would have figured out I wasn't at her apartment. She'd
have called my parents. But would they think I was just somewhere
in Hawaii?

Something gnawed at me.

The phones had been out.

What if they were still out? Did anyone on Midway wonder why
the plane hadn't arrived? My parents wouldn't know I'd been on it.
They'd think I was still in Hono.

I sighed.

So . . . no. If my parents were looking up at the sky, they weren't worried about me. They had no reason to be. Unless the phones were working and they'd tried to call.

Staring at the moon and the stars, I picked out a few constellations. Big Dipper. Little Dipper. Cassiopeia.

I thought about the ancient Polynesians, how they used the stars to navigate.

I sat up then, looking at the moon. The moon rose in the east.

I realized I had no idea which direction was which. I'd watched the sun set, and I knew that was west, but the raft was moving and I couldn't get my bearings. It sounded so easy to navigate by the sun and moon, but believe me, it was totally disorienting.

Was I anywhere near the Northwest Hawaiian Islands? I knew that there was nothing between Midway and other continents except for a few places like Johnston Atoll, Palmyra, and Wake Island. The chances of me reaching them with no food or water pretty much sucked.

But if we'd been north of the Northwest Hawaiian chain when we went down, then there were a lot of islands. At least the possibility of a lot of islands.

Laysan.

Pearl and Hermes.

French Frigate Shoals.

Lisianski.

Maybe I had a decent chance of reaching one of those. And, depending on where the G-1 ditched, and what direction the raft had traveled since then, I might not be that far away.

Settling down, closing my eyes, I vowed to pay attention in the morning when the sun rose, and try to steer the raft toward where I thought salvation might be. Or, if not rescue, at least water.

Water would be good.

I swallowed and the swallow, dry, stuck halfway down.

How long since I'd had to pee?

My eyes welled and a tear slipped down my cheek.

Water would be so good.

# thirty-two

On Day Three, I watched the sunrise. At least I thought it was the third day.

"What day is it, Max?"

His chin was on his chest and his eyes were closed. He didn't answer.

Since the sun rose in the east, I turned exactly opposite and mentally picked a point on the horizon to aim for. I scooted to the side of the raft and tried to paddle with my arm. The raft did move, but not with any efficiency. I couldn't reach both sides of the raft at the same time, so unless I moved from one side to the other between strokes, I would turn in circles eventually.

Plus, within minutes, I was out of breath. Lacking an actual paddle made the task too hard. Not to mention I was weaker than normal, and even my normal condition wasn't exactly athletic. Fortunately, it seemed like the raft was already heading in the direction I had wanted to go, so I just sat back, hoping the ocean current would get us somewhere before we starved or died of thirst. I held up my sweatshirt in the wind, thinking it might serve as a pseudo-sail, but it wasn't big enough to do much. And my arms were too tired to hold anything aloft for long.

A clump of something appeared about fifty yards away. I paddled again, trying to head toward it. As I got closer, I saw it was just a bunch of marine debris. The beaches at Midway were full of it. Every Sunday my parents and I picked the beaches to try to keep them clean for sea turtles and seals, but it was a losing battle. There was so much trash, a constant barrage, that we didn't make any difference.

For me, it had become a treasure hunt. Ask anyone on Midway, and the one thing they all wanted to find was a glass ball. Glass balls were actually old Japanese fishing floats. They used to be handblown, but then became factory produced before they stopped making them from glass altogether and switched to plastic. Shops in Honolulu sold them for a ton of money, and it was fun to find something for free that you knew tourists paid a lot of money for.

They were made of very sturdy glass, and I rarely saw a broken one, even though they had been floating around in the ocean for years and years. Some were small, the size of a baseball. But some were huge, the size of a basketball. I had a couple softball-size ones up on a shelf. I was always looking for those when we cleaned beaches. They were supposed to bring good luck.

So when I neared the batch of debris, I naturally looked for a glint of glass. We could use a little luck.

The smell of dead fish and rotten sea reached me before I got close enough to see what was in the debris. Covering my nose, I leaned over to look. Mainly a fishing net, with all its captured trash. An empty ketchup bottle, a soda can, each with Japanese writing. As far as I could tell, most ships in the Pacific just tossed their trash overboard. No wonder the oceans were in trouble.

A battered green toothbrush lay entwined in some of the net. My teeth felt like they'd grown fur and I *was* tempted . . . for about half a second.

Something red caught my eye. Without thinking, I reached out to snag it.

I let out a short laugh.

A fat, red-and-white plastic Santa Claus, both arms outstretched, with only one short stubby leg. Barnacles covered half of him, and a good deal of his paint was missing, but his jolly smile was still there. Along with his merry eyes.

"Maybe you'll be my luck."

Holding him to my chest, I grinned up at the sky where one white puffy cloud crept across the unbroken blue. But no others showed up to filter the blazing sun as the morning crept by.

I wanted to cry.

Hunger, thirst, pain from the infected piercing in my nose. And my lips. They were so dry I was afraid to move them. I forgot once, and licked them. My hands turned into fists until the stinging passed. I made a mental note not to ever lick my lips again.

I thought about *The Hunger Games*, how when the main character was about to give up, a little silver parachute would come floating down with exactly the item she needed.

At that moment, if I could have a silver parachute bring me anything, I would want some kind of lip balm. Well, no, that would be dumb. I needed food. Maybe some Power Bars. No, I wasn't supposed to eat if I didn't have water. So I'd want the silver parachute to bring water. A gallon of water. No, I'd use that up right away. I'd want a water purifier thing, so I could convert salt water to fresh water.

But was I going to get any of those things? No. There were no silver parachutes coming my way.

I sighed.

Some distraction from my situation would be really welcome.

Once again, I picked up the ditty bag. The Survival at Sea card was still crumpled in the bottom and I pulled it out, smoothing it down. "Okay, Survival at Sea dweebs, I'll give you another chance to help me survive." My voice was raspy. Maybe I should add talking out loud to the list of things I should no longer do. Except hearing my voice aloud was comforting for some reason. I liked it.

I skimmed past the Five Commandments of Survival.

**Sleep and rest are the best way to endure periods of reduced food and water.**

I gave myself a thumbs-up. Since I'd been doing little but sleeping and resting, I'd done one thing right at least.

Skimming over the section on water, which I'd already read, I noticed a small line under the part about the tarpaulin. A part I'd missed last time.

**A sponge can be used to collect dew off the raft.**

Dew?

"Are you serious?" I ran my hand along the edge of the raft, which was already bone dry from the sun. I groaned as I pulled the sponge out of the Coastal Commander and thwapped it against my forehead a couple of times.

If there was dew, I could have been getting moisture every morning.

*Tomorrow morning I'll be ready.*

I tucked the sponge away and read on to the section labeled Food.

**Eat any birds you can catch.**

Yeah. I would be sure to do that as soon as I caught one.

**Fish will be the main source of food at sea. Use your fishing gear to catch them.**

"Are you kidding me?" Right, let me grab my rod and reel.

Barely resisting the urge to toss the card into the sea, I kept reading.

**Fishing line and hook may be improvised from many materials.**

"Puhleeze." Just where was I going to find these materials? Setting the card down, I adjusted my hoodie under my butt, which was sore from sitting. And I noticed the string in the hood. Pulling on it, I managed to get it out. I held it up. Fishing line? Maybe.

But what about a hook?

I felt the silver hoops in my ears. Too flimsy.

What else was there?

I looked in the ditty bag. The spiral notebook?

I glanced over at Max.

Taking out the notebook, I twisted the metal until the end came out of the top. With my repeated twists, several inches stuck out. I bent it back and forth until about three inches of metal broke off. I held it up, and then curved it into a hook on one end. The other end I twirled around the string from my hood.

I smiled at my hook and line. "Who's inventive? Me. Totally."

Determined and hungry, I read on to see what else Survival at Sea could tell me about fishing.

**Do not handle the fishing line with bare hands or wrap it around your hands. Salt may adhere to it, making it a sharp cutting edge that could damage your hands or the raft.**

Eyeing the string from my hoodie, I didn't see how that could ever become sharp enough to hurt anything. I decided to ignore that part.

**Wear gloves in order to avoid injury from sharp fins.**

No gloves. But I could wrap my hands in my hoodie if I had to. I grinned at the card. "See? You keep trying to trip me up. But I've got you. I can do this."

**If you are in a warm area, gut and bleed fish right after you catch them.**

How was I going to do that? Even if I had a knife . . .

Any fish you do not eat right away must be cut into thin, narrow strips and hung to dry. A well-dried fish can stay edible for several days. Otherwise, fish may spoil in half a day, especially fish with dark meat. Do not eat any leftovers. Use any leftovers for bait.

*Bait.* My shoulders slumped. I had none and had no way to get any. I tossed the card aside. That was that.

My fishing was over before I even started.

# thirty-three

Morning turned to afternoon and I sat slumped in the raft, trying to sleep. But sleep didn't happen, so I just shaded my eyes and looked up at the sky. One fat, lazy cloud drifted above me. Soon, it was joined by another. Then many more began to move in, the clumps turning from puffy white to dark.

At first I was annoyed, because they obscured the sun, so that I couldn't be sure which way we were heading. Then, as a sprinkle hit my forehead, then another, and a shower began, I smiled. And when rain began to pour, I screamed with my hoarse voice, and then opened my mouth to the sky, drinking and swallowing.

Max was still sleeping, but there was rainwater gathering in the raft, so I figured I could scoop some up for him when he was ready.

And then I heaved, puking up all the water I'd just drunk.

I prayed the rain wouldn't stop, at least not until I had drunk my fill for the second time. A little more cautious, I kept my mouth open for a long time, swallowing, until my stomach felt full and my throat was no longer dry. My headache had gone away, and I pinched my hand, smiling as the skin sprang back quickly. No longer dehydrated.

Once again, I was soaked, but didn't care because I was too busy wondering how to catch the water. I did fill the bailer from the bottom of the raft, although there might have been a little bit of salt water remaining. Still, it would do when I got really thirsty again.

The rain didn't stop, and soon I was not only drenched but shivering, regretting my prayer for the rain not to stop. How quickly things went from one extreme to the other. I just wanted a happy medium, but wasn't even sure what that would be. A true happy medium would involve a sunny day and poolside service, but that was only a dream.

Even though I wasn't thirsty anymore, I forced myself to keep drinking periodically; the more I stored up, the better my body would handle another drought. And knowing the weather, the drought would probably come while I was still wet from the current deluge. But I drank so much I felt waterlogged, and there was a doubtful moment when I burped and began to wonder whether I would puke up everything again.

But I didn't. And when I was ready, I made myself drink more.

So I sat there, dripping wet and shaking, occasionally lifting my open mouth to the sky and drinking, waiting for the rain to end. And then Max woke, drank some rain, and told me more of his story.

"The morning after the cookies, I ran wind sprints in the wrestling room. All out—one end of the room to the other for forty-five minutes. I showed up at the scale and watched the numbers. One twelve point one."

My jaw dropped.

"Coach rolled his eyes and the ref started to write it down. I couldn't take it. So I stripped naked and stepped on again. One twelve."

I wanted to cheer, but I just smiled.

Max continued. "I took first in my weight. Then second at districts. Went to the state tournament seeded third. Getting a sixth-straight state title was on all of our minds. But we had to focus on our individual matches. That was the only way to get the state title."

"It sounds like a lot of pressure."

"I'd never been to Portland before. The bus ride took six hours. My first match went well. So did my second. At the semifinals, I waited for my opponent. He never showed. Instead, the ref walked over to me and raised my hand. The other kid got hurt and had to forfeit. I was in the finals."

I smiled. "That must have been a relief."

"I didn't sleep much that night," he continued, "and we had an early weigh-in. I was under, no problem, and immediately went to Denny's, where I chowed like I hadn't eaten in months."

I whispered, "Which you hadn't."

"My match was that night."

I couldn't imagine how nervous he must have been.

"When it was time, I stepped onto the mat. I wrapped the green cuff around my ankle. My opponent strapped the red one to his and stood eye to eye with me. We were the same size. His hair was short, like mine. But there was one big difference. He was a senior. And the reigning state champ."

I crossed my fingers for him and waited to hear the rest.

"I told myself, *Calm down, just do what you have to.* Three rounds stood between me and the podium. Three rounds of two minutes. Six minutes. That's it."

"That's it?" The match seemed so short to me.

He nodded. "Six minutes to be state champ. Focus on the first round. We crouched across from each other. Arms up, neutral position. We shook hands. From the look in his eyes, I knew that was the only sportsmanlike thing I could expect from him. The ref had a green band, my color, around his left wrist. I wanted to see that hand. I needed to see that hand up. A lot."

I hadn't watched much wrestling, but Max made it sound exciting.

"I was ready to shoot. Go for his legs. Try for a takedown. Time stopped, like it all was a snapshot. Like we'd been there forever. I glared at my opponent. He glared back. His eyes were blue. A zit on his chin needed popping. I squeezed my hands again, crouched lower, ready to spring as soon as I heard—"

I frowned. "What? Heard what?"

"The whistle. Like a bolt of lightning, he shot at my legs before I had a chance to go for his. I was on the defensive. I sprawled, hurling myself up and toward him. Hoping to get on top of him before he could get one of my legs. The crowd erupted. I knew it worked even before I had him on the ground."

"Yay!" I grinned.

"I had him in a cradle. It took everything I had to get one of his shoulders down. My face was in his armpit, his sweat rubbing off on me. I told myself, *Hold on! Hold on!*"

I silently chanted, *Hold on, Max, hold on, hold on. . . .*

"Coach yelled, 'Thirty!' I could do anything for thirty seconds, right? I could do anything for thirty seconds. I tried to get his other shoulder down, go for the pin." Max winced. "Round over. I glanced at the scoreboard. Zip–zip. There wasn't time to wonder why I hadn't gotten a point for the takedown. The ref tossed the coin. My opponent got to choose up or down to start the next round. He shook his head slightly, deferring to me. He wanted me to pick."

"Why?" I wondered aloud.

Max shrugged. "Psych-out tactic? Whatever. My legs were strong. I was usually up and out before anyone could touch me. Choosing down, I knelt on the mat. His breath was hot on my neck. I was ready to shove off from the mat, go up, and—"

I wondered aloud, "And what?"

"Before I could even move, his arm was looped under my arm and behind my neck in a half nelson and I was on my back."

"Oh." I assumed that was not a good position to be in.

"His fingers were like a vice. He had me."

"Was that it? Were you done?" I held my breath.

Max shook his head. "He had my left shoulder on the mat. The crowd screamed, but I blocked them out. Slowed everything down. There was only my pounding heart in my head. My legs, pushing and straining, trying to get out. My arms, one trying to push him, and the other still trying to get his fingers. Coach yelled, 'Twenty!' I could do anything for twenty seconds. He was going for the fall.

"The pin.

"The win.

"The state title.

"*I have got to move. Move! Move! Or I'm done!*

"But he's got me. He's got me."

"Max . . . oh no . . ." I breathed out.

"The ref slams his hand against the mat. The crowd explodes. Pinned. I'm still on my back. My opponent throws his headgear into the air. He lets the ref hold up his arm in victory and starts jumping around the mat, screaming. I lay there, hands over my face. I wanted to . . . to . . ."

"What?" I asked.

"I wanted to cry," he said. "But I didn't."

## thirty-four

Max stopped, leaned back against the raft, and shut his eyes.

My heart was pounding and I took a few deep breaths.

There was more to tell, I knew, but I could wait. We had plenty of time.

The rain had stopped, but the wind had grown stronger. The raft surged along in the waves, which were higher than they'd been since the storm. I was so used to the movement by then that I wasn't frightened like I usually would have been in a boat. And I wasn't feeling the fear I'd felt the first day or two. Anxiety had transitioned to boredom. Just sitting there, watching the same sky, same water, same colors. I longed for something to break up the monotony.

I opened my eyes.

Something moved in the sky, coming closer.

*Is that what I think it is?*

It was.

I inhaled softly and tears came to my eyes.

A black-and-white Laysan albatross was directly above me, wings straight out and motionless, soaring effortlessly in the wind. For all I knew, it was one of the gooney birds from Midway, one of those who nested in my front yard.

"Hello, gooney bird!" Grinning, I raised both arms in the air and hugged myself.

Funny, all those stories about shipwrecks and people lost at sea, they always wanted to see a bird, because it meant land couldn't be far off. But the albatross didn't raise any such hopes in me. Albatross were capable of traveling thousands of miles to bring food back for their chicks. They ate squid eggs or fish and, once they got back to their nest, regurgitated it for the chicks in an oily, viscous, vile-smelling substance.

That albatross was a little piece of home. The life cycle of the albatross was something I got to experience every year on Midway. From August until October, Midway was void of albatross. The fields were empty, as were the skies. Then, beginning in October, they started coming back. Sighting the first albatross of the season was a game the whole island played. I would ride my bike all over, looking. Then, one day, over the radio, we'd hear, "The albatross are back!" And we'd all race in our bicycles or golf carts to where the first birds had been spotted.

At first, there were a couple in a field, dotting the empty space. But within a week or two, the air was full of them, and soon after every available inch of unpaved open ground and grass had a nest. Albatross mate for life, which can be up to seventy years. They build their nest in the same spot every year. And they dance. A very specific dance, with eighteen actual moves, consisting of dips and bows and calls to the sky. They look so goofy doing it that troops stationed on Midway during World War II nicknamed them gooney birds. We just called them gooneys.

Along with the dancing came screeching. So much that some people on Midway slept with earplugs when the gooneys were dancing. I never did though. I liked all the noise and became so used to it, I almost didn't hear it anymore. Actually, I was kind of bothered by the people who saw the sound as a nuisance. It was a part of nature not that many people got to experience.

One sound I loved was the albatross parents talking to their eggs, a reassuring and melodic *eh eh eh*. Sometimes an egg wouldn't hatch, and long after all the other eggs had hatched, the parents still talked to the dead egg.

Hoping, maybe.

The same thing happened when a chick died. The adults would still talk to it. Then, one day, they would be gone.

Because they knew somehow when it was time to give up. To stop hoping.

The gooney hovered above me, curious.

The line of the Survival at Sea card came to me, the one about killing any bird you see.

But this albatross was no bird. Not to me.

Albatross had souls.

As hungry as I was, I knew too much about albatross, had seen how they lived.

Supposedly albatross had the ability to sleep while they were aloft, to shut down a part of their brains in order to allow themselves rest while on their long flights.

I wondered what this one was doing, how far it had been flying. Where it was going. Was it a parent with a chick somewhere?

It was mid-June, rather late in the season for parents to still be feeding their chicks. By now, they'd given up, tired of it, ready to take off until it was time to start the cycle all over.

Could it be one of this season's chicks? This was the time of year when they left their nesting grounds to be on their own.

Chicks learned to live, or die, by flying out to sea.

And, if they survived, they stayed out at sea for seven years before coming back to Midway to nest. We called them teenagers, the ones who were back at Midway for the first few years, because they didn't really know what to do. They danced in groups, trying to find a mate. And sometimes they did pair up and build a nest and lay an egg. But often they wouldn't know what to do with it.

The egg had to be kept warm, had to be nestled constantly for sixty days.

When I'd go by a nest and see both parents sitting beside the nest, looking at the egg, I'd know they were teenagers, trying to figure it out. And of course they always did, eventually. But not soon enough for that year's egg.

A few drops of moisture fell on me from the gooney's wings as it circled over me and came around again.

Had it ever seen people on the ocean before? Of course, in ships. But like this? Such a small patch of raft, so low to the water?

*Does it wonder what we are? Why we're here?*

The bird passed over me, continuing on its way. However old, or young, it was, the gooney seemed content in its world of sky and sea. The raft was simply a momentary distraction.

I waved good-bye, watching until tears blurred my vision and I could see it no more.

Late afternoon lowered the sun, which made the clouds moving to the east look especially purplish and dark. When I looked that way, I saw something in the distance. Something weird. Almost like a blur, kind of in the shape of a tornado, but a whitish and constantly shifting form in the sunlight.

As it came closer, I saw them. And heard them.

Birds. An agitated, chaotic, screeching cloud of birds. I picked out the ones I knew. Sooty terns, at least one blue-footed booby, a few fairy terns. They shifted and dove and flew. Below them, the surface of the water showed just as much, if not more, commotion.

I'd seen that before, when I'd gone fishing at Midway with my dad. The birds followed the small fish, trying to catch them, as below, larger fish tried to eat the smaller ones. It was how we knew where to drop our fishing lines.

What did they call it?

I snapped my fingers. *Bait ball.* And this bait ball was heading straight for the raft. A whole lot of fish were coming right to me.

"Max!"

He didn't move.

My hands started to shake as my heart thumped.

I could get a fish.

I could get a fish, eat some of it, and then use the rest for bait to get more. I couldn't stop myself from licking my parched lips.

The Survival at Sea people could shove it.

*I can do this.*

Every year, a fairy tern always laid her egg right on the railing of our front porch. The chick was just a little white ball of puff, no taller than two or three inches to start. I'd named this year's chick Sméagol, because I'd just reread *Lord of the Rings.*

The mother brought back small flying fish, sometimes so big the fish dwarfed Sméagol. I knew there had to be some of those little flying fish in that bait ball, and with any luck . . .

The smaller fish jumped right out of the water where any bird worth its feathers snatched them up. As they came nearer, I wondered whether I could use my hoodie as a net, either to scoop some out or catch them as they jumped. I took it in both hands and stretched it out, then doubled my grip. Everything depended on whether or not they avoided the raft.

Kneeling, poised with my hoodie in trembling hands, I held my breath as the edge of the bird cloud reached me. All the calls and cries and screeches were a cacophony after so much silence. The small fish were so close I could almost reach out and touch them. Something warm and sticky plopped on my head. Then on my shoulder.

Bird poop.

Like a reflex, my nose scrunched, causing me to wince in pain. As I did, several of the little flying fish jumped up, so close, and with my hoodie I swatted them down into the raft, where they flopped on the bottom.

"Yes!" I hooted. "Take that SURVIVAL AT FRICKIN' SEA! Woohoo!"

The bait ball seemed to stall over me, and I put the hoodie over my head to ward off the assault of the birds. Their cries continued as I watched the small fish die. Too bad. I needed them.

One of the fish finally stopped thrashing right next to the plastic Santa Claus. As I reached for it, the Santa Claus jumped about six inches off the bottom of the raft.

I fell back as something bumped my butt, shoving me upward.

"Oh, God."

Something was under the raft. Something big.

# thirty-five

I tried to see into the water. There were small fish and larger shapes under them, a couple feet long, which were probably tuna or wahoo or ulua. But under those? Could be anything. The guys who fished on Midway sometimes complained of Galapagos sharks trailing them, stealing their fish just as they try to haul them aboard.

Another bump from under.

*Crap.*

I stopped trying to look. My hands began to shake. Maybe I didn't want to know.

*Please don't tip over the raft.*

I picked up one of the little flying fish. If I didn't get tipped over and eaten, I would still be hungry.

I grabbed my hook and stuck the fish on.

"Sorry, little guy."

Gripping the line, I wrapped it once around my fist and tossed it over.

The line was short, about two feet, so the fish was barely in the water. Immediately, there was a tug. On Midway we fished with huge reels attached to the back of boats. But I'd been fishing for small stuff with a rod before on my grandparents' lake in Wisconsin. I knew enough to wait, let them set the hook in their mouth, then yank. I waited.

Another tug.

I yanked.

The fish yanked back and the raft began to move. It was all I could do to hang on. I had a good-size one.

Sitting back down so I could use my whole body's weight, I held tight. I wished I'd remembered to wrap the hoodie around it, just in case the line did end up being sharp enough to cut through my skin. But it was too late, so the only thing to do was hold on as best as I could.

One fist at a time, I started pulling the line in. The striped face of a yellow skipjack appeared above the water, its eyes shiny and dark. The sight gave me more strength and I pulled harder. The fish was almost all the way above water, and I grinned, even though I had no idea how I was going to gut the thing.

"Oh man! Max, I caught a—"

The words died as a big open mouth with rows of razor-sharp teeth burst out of the water just below the skipjack and snapped shut, taking a mouthful of water and most of the fish below the waves. The shark was gone almost before I'd registered what happened.

I let out a belated but still startled shriek.

As hard as I'd been pulling, the force brought the rest of the skipjack into my lap. I quickly shoved it off, onto the floor of the raft where it lay, bloody, next to the Santa and the other little flying fish.

Another bump under my butt made me shriek louder.

"Get out of here!" I started waving my hands, shooing the birds, hoping maybe if they moved, the bait ball would leave, and take that shark with it. "Go! Go away!"

Within seconds, the birds had moved off, and the surface of the water no longer churned. The bait ball had moved on.

My gaze went to the mangled skipjack, who stared up at me with glazed, lifeless eyes. Well, the shark had done me one favor. I no longer had to worry about how to gut the thing.

I blew out the breath I didn't even know I'd been holding. My thirst wasn't at the point where I was desperate enough to try eating the eyeballs or sucking the spinal fluid.

Skipjack was in the tuna family, and I liked sashimi, which was raw tuna. It couldn't be that different, could it?

The fish was slippery and slid right out of my hands. Then I picked it back up and cradled it with one arm against my chest. My white camisole was already filthy; a few fish guts wouldn't make it any worse.

I dug out a piece of pink flesh with my fingers.

"It's just sashimi." Although my mom always let the tuna rest in the fridge for a day before she cut and served it, I didn't have that luxury, and with the sun going down before too long, I might not be able to even dry it in time. If I wanted to eat that day, I would have to eat that fish. Raw.

*Sashimi. Just sashimi.*

I popped the morsel into my mouth and chewed. The fish was slimy and salty and I started to gag, but managed to swallow.

"Not that bad." Saying it out loud didn't make it any more real. But I dug in for another piece and ate that too. Trying to distract myself, so I wasn't totally focused on the dead fish in my lap, I decided to count my blessings.

I'd caught a fish. I'd actually caught a fish.

Another good thing? Catching the fish in the open ocean meant I wouldn't have to worry about diseases I could catch from eating reef fish. Like ciguatera. Fish caught the toxin by eating small reef creatures and cooking didn't even kill the poison.

Ciguatera brought nausea, vomiting, and diarrhea. And after

those symptoms, neurological ones set in, like the loss of coordination and a constant feeling of pins and needles.

Nasty. And pretty much incurable too.

I popped another piece of fish in my mouth. Yup, I was very happy to be eating from the ocean.

My stomach gurgled.

I swallowed and paused. Maybe my poor shrunken tummy was just happy to be getting some protein after three days of nothing but a few off-colored Skittles. I continued eating, hoping Max would wake up so he could have some too. I considered trying to rouse him.

But I didn't.

I kept eating until I was so stuffed, I burped.

I set aside the rest of the fish for Max, hoping he'd wake up soon to eat something. But it didn't take long for what remained of the skipjack to smell. The only smart thing to do would be to get rid of it, because as soon as I got hungry again, I'd be tempted. I threw the remains as far away from the raft as I could and washed my hands in the salt water. I lay back against the side of the raft and tried to adjust to the full feeling in my stomach.

It wasn't very hard to do. Then Max woke up. If he knew I'd eaten, he didn't say anything about it. And I didn't mention it. I just listened.

## thirty-six

Max sounded so determined. "I refused to come that close ever again without winning. I started eating again. Over the summer, I grew about five inches and put on thirty pounds."

"Wow, that's a lot." I guiltily stifled another burp. "But how did you get back to one twelve?"

"After that I wrestled one thirty-five and was state champ the next two years."

I smiled. "Congratulations."

"Wrestling wasn't everything. She meant more to me. I would have given it up for her. I would have given anything up for her."

I wondered who *she* was.

Max told me. "Brandy Thomas and I started going out sophomore year. Kinda weird, since I'd known her since kindergarten, when she wore her black hair in braids."

Growing up as I had, that was hard for me to imagine. I hadn't known anyone since kindergarten. Sometimes I missed that, having classmates I had known forever. Was it odd to miss something I'd never had?

Max went on. "Sophomore year, the girls who had been about my height were suddenly shorter than I was. They saw me differently. I saw me differently. I'd never dated, not even prom."

I'd never dated. I'd never even talked to a boy, really, other than a couple I met at AJ's pool. Would I ever get the chance to date? I realized a tear was trickling down my face and I quickly wiped it away.

Max smiled. "When homecoming came up, my friends kept telling me to ask someone out. Brandy and I had always been friendly. She lived out on the reservation and was quiet, but funny. Very opinionated. Good in school. A few weeks before homecoming our sophomore year, I walked up to her at her locker and asked her to homecoming. That was it. Neither of us ever dated anyone else."

I smiled. Max sounded so in love.

"Brandy's mom never liked me that much."

I wondered how she could possibly not like him. I barely knew him, but I could just tell he was a good person.

"I was always polite. But she didn't trust me with her daughter. I could tell. Maybe she had a feeling, an intuition. Maybe she knew something we didn't."

I wasn't sure what that meant, but Max didn't say anything else.

## thirty-seven

Evening came and I took stock. Max was asleep again. With all I'd had to eat, I felt so much better. I even had to pee for the first time in a while. But I was still sunburned, and the piercing in my nose was hurting more and more.

And I was still stuck in a raft in the middle of nowhere.

Clouds covered up the stars and moon, making the night very black. I took out the Coastal Commander, extracted the flashlight, and turned it on. The immediate area of the raft lit up as I shone the light around me and checked on Max. I clicked it off, and black swallowed everything. That dark was even worse than before.

So I clicked it back on.

I couldn't keep turning the flashlight off and on all night. I held a flare in my hand. It would be a waste. I needed to save those in case I heard a plane or a boat. Fumbling in the dark, I stuck everything back in the Coastal Commander and fastened it into its pocket.

Then I laid my head on the side of the raft and tried to sleep. The water was calm, pushing us up and down so slightly I barely noticed.

I'd grown used to the motion.

And the quiet. At first, the quiet was so loud. There was so much nothing that I couldn't block it out. But I was getting used to that too, the quiet. Which is probably why, when I dozed off, the distant sound woke me up.

My eyes blinked in the darkness, straining to see. The sound didn't register at first and it took me a moment to break it down.

A drone.

I knew that sound. It was a C-130.

The Coast Guard.

*Rescue.*

I waved both my arms. "Hey! Hey!"

*Stupid. Like they could hear or see you.*

The flares. I needed the flares.

"Max! A plane!"

Patting with my hands in the dark, I found the pocket and unzipped it, then pulled out the Coastal Commander. I turned on the flashlight and shone it into the bag, then pulled out a flare. Was it like the one Max had used? I held it closer so I could read the directions. From what I could tell, I just needed to strip off the wax seal and pull the string.

*How long had Max's flare lasted?*

*Should I wait until the plane sounded closer?*

It still sounded far away.

There were more flares. I could use this one as a demo, and then wait until the plane was closer to fire up another.

I propped the flashlight in my mouth so I could use both hands, then peeled the wax off the top of the flare. I held it out in one hand, pulled the string, and then pointed it away from the raft. I flicked off the flashlight and waited for the fireworks.

I heard a low hiss and some puffing. But there was no light.

A slight breeze picked up and I couldn't breathe. Coughing and choking, I switched hands, pointed the flare downwind, and turned the flashlight on.

Orange smoke. That was the only thing flooding out of the flare. Nothing but orange smoke. Heaving the flare into the water, I swore.

I'd lit the wrong kind. A smoke flare was for daytime.

I shone the flashlight back in the bag. Two left. I was more careful about reading the labels. One was another smoke signal flare so the other had to be the real kind. I pulled it out and readied myself, waiting until the plane came closer.

So I sat there, heartbeat pulsing in my ears, hands shaking.

"Come on, come on."

The drone grew closer, although with the cloudy sky, I still couldn't see any lights and had no way of telling how close it truly was. Then I couldn't wait any longer. I hoped the flare would go for at least ten minutes, maybe more. And that C-130 sounded like it was only a minute or two away.

I put the flashlight in my mouth and got up on my knees. I peeled off the wax, said a silent prayer, and pointed the flare toward the direction of the plane. I pulled the fuse and held out the flare with one hand, keeping the other tight on the side of the raft.

Sparks flew out and with a great rushing whistle, the flare went off. And up. The cylinder in my hand was empty.

All the fireworks followed an arc up into the sky where they lasted about ten seconds then dispersed into small stars trickling back down.

My mouth dropped open, and the flashlight fell into the water. "No!" I grabbed for it but was too late, and could only watch the light spiral down and around, down and around, growing fainter and fainter, then finally fading away.

With engines roaring, the C-130 burst through the clouds overhead, red lights blinking.

"Hey! I'm down here!" I waved my arms.

But the plane didn't slow.

The pilot didn't dip his wings in acknowledgment.

No one dropped out in a parachute.

Because they didn't see me. They didn't know the raft was there.

I set my arms on my head, elbows up, fingers clasped together at the back of my head. I breathed out.

I wasn't getting saved. Not that night.

The C-130 disappeared as quickly as it had appeared.

Dropping my arms, I clutched myself.

Within a minute or so, the C-130's drone faded out to nothing, returning my world to a soundless, lightless void.

I managed one halfhearted "come back!"

Then I curled up in the dark and cried.

## thirty—eight

I awoke to a drizzle and rolled onto my back, letting what drops of rain there were fall into my open mouth. After the disaster of the night before, I had no energy to do more. Max hadn't moved. I didn't have the heart to tell him about the plane. Or how I'd failed to signal it.

After a while, I sat up. Directly in front of me, I thought I saw a line on the horizon.

It could have just been a low cloud bank. The day was overcast, so the lack of visibility and my own exhaustion could have been playing tricks on me.

As the day went on, the line got slightly bigger. There was definitely something there. I wanted Max to wake up so I could show him. See what he thought it might be.

And just then, he woke up. He took a few moments to orient himself, and then he clung to the side of the raft and looked skyward, opening his mouth and drinking. Water dripped down his face and he didn't bother to wipe it away.

I didn't tell him about the C-130. Instead, I pointed to the line on the horizon. "Do you think that's an island?"

We both stared in that direction for a few minutes.

Max squinted. "Could be." Exactly what I had been thinking.

The sun came out now and then. Near the end of the day, we drew ever nearer to the line, and it had become something real. I noticed the clouds above it were green, which meant they were reflecting the color of water, shallower water, which meant a reef and an island.

And then the birds came.

Fairy terns, sooty terns, a few brown noddies. This time, they weren't part of a bait ball. This time, they were close to home.

The line was definitely an island. And we were getting nearer every minute.

I had a few ideas as to what island it could be. Or couldn't be. Or hoped it wouldn't be.

Laysan was a possibility. It was the time of year when researchers would be there, so that would be perfect. But I was pretty sure Laysan was too far to the east of where we probably were.

Pearl and Hermes Atoll, also probably too far.

The Gardner Pinnacles were a possibility, but they would suck. Basically just two pieces of tall rock, they were great for birds and insects, no place for humans. And I didn't see anything of much height, so it couldn't be that anyway.

As I strained my memory, trying to picture a map of the area, I kept coming back to the name of Lisianski Island. I was pretty sure it was in the area. And it wouldn't be bad at all. Having spent the last few years in the company of adults, I'd learned to make myself a little more viable during long dinner conversations involving mainly biologists and other scientists. I had scoured the Internet and memorized a bunch of cool, gross, or amazing facts about some of the more obscure Northwest Hawaiian Islands, guaranteeing myself at least some attention at the dinner table.

And there were a few facts about Lisianski that I always remembered.

Sometime in the early 1900s rabbits had been introduced to the island, where they had multiplied, of course—they were rabbits. But the food supply eventually ran out and they become cannibals, the old devouring the young. A naturalist visiting the island from Honolulu reported seeing the last newborn rabbit being eaten alive by the last starving mother.

Hard to forget something like cannibal rabbits.

Plus my mom had a fit when I told that story at the dinner table. She sent me to my room right before she served my favorite dessert, Better than Anything cake.

I sighed just picturing it.

German chocolate cake, poked with holes that were then filled with an entire can of sweetened condensed milk. Then the whole cake was covered with caramel ice cream sauce, spread with Cool Whip, and topped off with crushed Heath bars. Even more of a reason not to forget the evening or the cannibal rabbits of Lisianski.

Lisianski was also pretty well known for bird poaching. About the same time as the rabbits, law enforcement raided the island and discovered poachers with the feathers of over 140,000 dead birds.

*Sick.*

I wondered if the women wearing feathered hats or people sleeping on feather beds, resting their heads on down pillows ever thought about where the filler came from. How many birds went extinct just so they could have a soft place to lay their head?

Luckily for the birds, Teddy Roosevelt declared the whole area the Hawaiian Island Bird Reservation. Since then it became protected in other ways, and under other names, and Lisianski was once again loaded with birds.

All in all, Lisianski wouldn't be a bad place to end up. Certainly not the worst. And way better than being stuck in a raft.

The sun was close to setting when I heard waves crash. Since I'd been on the raft, the waves hadn't made sound. Even the big ones, with deep troughs, were relatively quiet. So hearing those waves crash could only mean one thing: an island or reef close by.

My heart beat faster.

My only experience with a reef was at Midway. We would take the boat out there to see Hawaiian monk seals and spinner dolphins. All was calm and beautiful inside the reef, but outside, where the ocean crashed against it, was deadly. Midway had an opening in its reef where ships could go through. But the rest of it? Solid. Ships had been wrecked on the reef. Reefs are coral, which is sharp. The reef would rip the raft to pieces if it got smashed against it. Hell, the reef would rip *me* to pieces if I got smashed against it.

Could I decide what to do on my own?

I sighed and clasped my hands behind my head as I considered my options. *Option,* really. Because there wasn't really any going around it. Our best chance of survival was to be out of the raft and on that island, whatever island it was.

My gaze went to Max. The raft would be lighter with neither of us in it, and might even just skim over the reef on one good wave. But we might not survive getting bashed against the reef on our own. We needed to go over with the raft if at all possible.

The line of the island was closer. I sat on my haunches, hands gripping the front of the raft, watching as a wave lifted us. I screamed as we headed straight for the reef.

## thirty-nine

Up. I went up.
 And then down.
 I was out of the raft.
 Falling.
 So slow.
 Was I flying?
 There was green.
 And then gray. And brown.
 Gray and white and brown.
 Reef.
 Sudden pain. *My head!*
 And then nothing.

forty

*Clack! Clack! Clack!*

I moaned. My head felt split in two.

*Clack! Clack!*

I was lying facedown on the sand, my arms stretched out on either side. I tried to blink, and then scrunched my eyes as I realized my face, along with the rest of my body, was packed with sand. I brushed off my face, but cried out when I touched my left eye.

I couldn't see on that side.

I tried again to blink. But only my right eye worked.

*Clack! Clack! Clack!*

Feeling gingerly with my fingers, I discovered my left eye was swollen. So swollen.

My mouth was all gritty and I spit, tried to work up some saliva, then spit again.

How had I gotten to shore?

A rough wave lifted me slightly, started to pull me back out, but my body stopped abruptly as I felt a pulling on my hair.

Turning a bit, I realized my hair had gotten entwined in the succulent green naupaka bushes lining the beach. I tried not to think about what would have happened if a wave had taken me back out when I was still unconscious on my belly.

I owed the naupaka a big thank-you.

*Clack! Clack! Clack!*

Without pulling on my hair, I turned my head so my right eye was aimed up the bank.

Several young gooneys stood there, black-and-white adult feathers peeking through their silvery baby down in spots. They glared at me, the clacking of their beaks the only way they had to let me know they were pissed off at my sudden intrusion on their beach.

Ignoring them, I got to work on freeing myself.

My fingers were wrinkled and wet and had cuts on them. I tried to untangle my hair. I must have been lying there for a while, because several of my cornrows were completely twisted in the plant. I tried to unbraid them, to no avail.

The raft.

Max.

I called for him, but as I tried to stand, the bushes held firm. So, grimacing at the pain, I started yanking until I was free. Feeling with my fingers, I found one decent-sized bald spot. It was just hair. A small price to pay for being alive and on an island.

*On an island!*

I needed to find Max.

My legs threatened to buckle beneath me. Weaving a bit, I staggered through the naupaka and up the bank, scattering the albatross, which retreated but continued their constant clacking.

Being blind on the left required me to move slowly, gain my balance. Having been on the raft for so long didn't help either.

Reaching the top of the bank, I stood above the beach, scanning for any sign of Max. "Max?" I called for him, and then noticed something yellow down the beach, about a hundred yards. The raft. "Max!"

Jumping back down to the beach, my legs gave out and I landed on my belly, knocking my breath into the sand. I lay there for a second and summoned any strength I had left.

Getting slowly back up on my feet, I moved unsteadily. The raft was there, shredded by the coral reef, but still in one piece, more or less. There was no chance it would ever hold air again, that was for sure. The left side had been ripped away and the Coastal Commander was gone. The ditty bag was nowhere to be seen either. I struggled to pull the raft up off the beach.

Shading my one good eye, I looked out in the water. Nothing.

My legs buckled and I fell to the sand. It didn't mean anything. Max could still be okay. I made it. He could too. Crawling onto what was left of the raft, I lay down and slept.

When I woke, I felt better, although my left eye was still swollen shut and my head throbbed. I sat up slowly, and felt on my way to getting used to being on solid land again. My body still felt like it was swaying though, as if I was still on the water.

I looked around.

The island was small, that's for sure, and if I had to guess, I'd say it was probably Lisianski. Which meant at least I had gone from being in the middle of nowhere to a place that was actually on the map. Definitely an improvement.

Some of the smaller islands in the area didn't have scientists on them during the summer, but they did get checked on periodically by research ships as they passed. So there was a pretty good chance someone would pass by this island. And I intended to be ready when they did.

My stomach growled. I had to find something to eat.

Sooty terns flew overhead, their cries raucous and their bellies green from the reflection of the sun off the water. More Internet trivia popped into my head: The soundtrack of the birds from Alfred Hitchcock's movie *The Birds* was actually sooty terns recorded on Eastern Island at Midway. It was nice to hear life around me after all those days and nights of quiet.

My stomach growled again.

With all the birds, there had to be eggs on the island. But even if I did get the nerve up to eat one, there was no way to cook them.

I stubbed my toe and reached down to pick up the blue culprit. A plastic cigarette lighter. I opened my hand and let it drop back to the sand. There were thousands of them on the beaches at Midway, and looking around, I saw them everywhere. Useless.

Although hungry and thirsty, I needed to prioritize. In case a plane flew over or a ship went by, I needed to be able to signal them. And I didn't have any flares. I headed unsteadily toward the center of the island where two dunes rose in a V-shape about thirty feet high.

I climbed to the top and plopped down, breathing hard. Water as far as I could see around the island. The breeze lifted my hair a bit as the sun stung my sunburned face. Green sea turtles dozed on the beach and an involuntary smile crept upon my face as I wiped the sand off my ankle. The tattoo was still visible. The fact that it looked so good, the henna so dark, the drawing so pristine, made it seem completely out of place on my wreck of a body. I sighed and looked down the beach. Another sea turtle had joined the rest.

Sea turtles spent a lot of time on Midway, but they didn't lay eggs there. I wondered if this island was one where they did. The turtles looked huge, even from as far away as I was. They were a species that had my respect, to even be able to survive. The females sometimes went to sea for twenty-five years before laying eggs.

I slid down the sand to the bottom, landing near a small pile of driftwood. A signal fire made the most sense, except there was no way for me to light it.

I pushed a small log over and it rolled down the small incline.

Another cigarette lighter, orange this time, lay there. I picked it up. How easy would that be, to have a cigarette lighter to light my signal fire?

With my thumb, I flicked the wheel. Nothing. The mechanism was so rusty, it didn't budge even a tad. I shook the lighter, and the liquid inside sloshed.

Lighter fluid? Or seawater?

Another lighter, blue, lay within reach, and I picked it up. Again there was liquid inside. If I found enough of them with lighter fluid, I could break them open and pour all the fluid on a pile of wood. Then I would only need to find one that actually worked. It was like buying a lottery ticket. Eventually I had to win something, right?

At least it was something to do.

Picking up the wood from the small pile, I carried it to the top of the dune, the best place for a signal fire. For about an hour, I hunted for wood, chose only the driest pieces, and ended up with a pretty good-size pile on top of the dune. A faded green plastic fishing float broken in two served well as a bucket as I went around collecting lighters. The float didn't take long to fill, and I carried it back to the raft.

Max was there, sitting on what was left of it.

# forty-one

My mouth fell open. "How are you here?" I asked.

He shrugged. "How are *you* here?"

I glanced out at the reef, where waves crashed into the outside. The same waves that had slammed the raft.

"Good question."

The odds of someone making it to the beach after such a beating were probably pretty low. I touched my left eye. Maybe I was lucky to come through as unscathed as I had. I sat down beside him.

Max didn't look that bad. I was glad not to be alone and I told him my plan.

I picked up a lighter and flicked the wheel, hoping for a flame. A spark. Some sign that it still worked. One by one, I went through my bucketful.

Disappointed every time, I tossed the rejects into a pile to be broken later, any fluid left in them to be poured on my signal fire. When I got to the bottom of the pile, I kicked the empty fishing float away.

"There are a lot more lighters," said Max. "You only need one to get lucky."

I nodded. "I'm not giving up. Just taking a break." Off to the west, clouds gathered. "Maybe rain." I picked up the fishing float to check for holes. To get rain, I'd have to set out some containers. I set off to see what I could find that would hold water.

I walked the beach around the bend, until I couldn't see Max or the raft. Only after about ten minutes did I realize how tired I was. I found a warm, clean patch of sand and sat down, just for a moment's rest. The sun was so warm, I lay back and shut my good eye.

A raucous croaking sound woke me.

I sat up. Too quickly, because I felt light-headed for a moment.

The sound continued, sounding like a massive, low-toned frog.

As I neared a dune, the sound was louder and I dropped to my knees and lay on top, so I could peek without being seen. Roughly thirty yards down the beach, a Hawaiian monk seal about six feet long with a dark coat lay with its back to me. The seal, more slender than most I'd seen, faced the water, calling and calling.

By the size of it, I figured the seal was female.

I glanced out where her gaze was focused, but didn't notice anything.

There were Hawaiian monk seals at Midway, which was critical habitat for them, a place they needed in order to survive. Because with only about 1,300 monk seals left in the world, extinction was a very real possibility. So most of the beaches at Midway were off-limits to humans. If we did stumble upon a seal, we were supposed to stay a hundred yards away, and you risked getting sent packing if you disobeyed the rules.

Most of the time they just lay there on the beach, snoozing away, oblivious to any humans peering at them through a lens. I didn't see how hiding behind napaka watching them was any more harmful than the stupid seal researchers catching them and taking blood samples. To me, that seemed way more traumatizing.

The seal cried out again. But the cry held something else this time. It was hard to tell, but the sound that came out of her mouth sounded like pain. And then she rolled onto her back.

I gasped and slapped a hand over my mouth. I whispered, *"Sick."*

Her belly was slashed open, bleeding, with innards exposed and tumbling out.

The only thing that could do that kind of damage was a shark.

## forty-two

Immediately, I looked out into the lagoon, but saw nothing in the water. The seal could have been fishing outside of the lagoon when it happened. That made more sense. Although with all the young albatross on the island leaving, or getting ready to leave, there probably were tiger sharks around. A lot of them.

My arms broke out in goose bumps.

The seal cried again. She tried to roll back the other way, but she got stuck. Then I saw one of her flippers had been bitten completely off. I don't know how she even managed to make it ashore. Or why the shark didn't finish her off.

Tears filled my right eye as I watched her suffer.

There was nothing I could do. Even if we'd been closer to civilization, closer to a marine mammal facility with specialized vets and equipment, I don't know what they could do to help her.

We were in the middle of nowhere with nothing. And she was not going to heal on her own. She couldn't grow another flipper.

Her cries dimmed, until they were raspy whimpers. She was in so much pain.

Tears spilled down my cheeks, even eking out from my bad eye.

*Think. Figure it out.*

I thought about what would have happened if this had been Midway. The biologist would have had to call the National Marine

Fisheries Service in Honolulu, because they were in charge of the monk seals and their habitat.

And then?

The NMFS would have told them what to do.

Which was what?

Midway had no vet, no one qualified to operate. Even the medical person there for humans wasn't qualified for that. Glancing again at her injuries, I doubted anyone anywhere knew how to fix her. Factor in the NMFS not being able to reach Midway for at least half a day, and there wasn't much anyone on Midway could have done to help her.

With the back of my hand, I wiped off my tears and stood up.

It wasn't in me to sit and watch her die.

Retreating down the dune, I began looking for something. Something hard and heavy.

A few pieces of driftwood lay strewn about on the beach, but they looked too light. In a bigger pile of marine debris, I found a broken board. As I hefted it, I knew that the board, combined with my current level of adrenaline and emotion, would work.

Still sniffling, I climbed back to the top of the dune and knelt.

The seal was moaning now, or what seemed like moaning. As close to human as an animal sound could get.

It was cruel, so cruel, to make her suffer when I could do something about it.

I couldn't wait anymore.

She no longer faced me, so I walked quickly but softly until I was a few feet away. A slight breeze brushed my face.

I breathed in and got her smell.

A little fishy.

Salty.

She *was* the ocean.

Gripping the board in both hands, I lifted both arms over my head and steeled myself, gathering all my energy. I wanted to have to hit her only once because I didn't know whether I could make myself do it a second time.

Just as I was ready to bring the board down, her head fell my way, both of her eyes looking up at mine. There was no surprise in her gaze. Like she expected me to be there. To help her.

As she looked at me, I swear she was crying.

"I'm so sorry . . ."

Then I cried out as I brought the board down as hard as I could.

## forty-three

Tossing the board away, I sunk to my knees beside her, not even caring that she could rip into me if she was still alive.

But she wasn't, that was clear. Nothing about her whispered life. Brushing past her whiskers, I held a hand in front of the slits that were her nostrils.

She wasn't suffering anymore. But she had been one of only a few of her kind.

Endangered.

Harming an endangered animal resulted in fines of hundreds of thousands of dollars. Jail. I'd done way worse than *harm*. But I'd had no choice.

I set a hand on her head. Her eyes were still open.

Still full of tears.

Still so sad.

Still so . . . human.

With gentle hands, I closed them for her.

As I sat there beside her, my legs crossed, I reached out and lightly stroked her side.

I'd never touched a seal before.

Her dark skin was slick, smooth. I stroked her face, ran my fingers across her whiskers. "It's okay now. You're okay."

Shaking my head, I wiped my eyes and looked out at the water.

Something moved in the waves.

Or it could have been my imagination.

Yet there it was again.

Something round.

A head.

A black shiny head.

Coming right toward me. No. Not toward me. Toward the seal.

"Oh, no. No. No, no, no."

*It couldn't be.*

Getting to my feet, I scrambled for the dune, diving out of sight. Then I crawled on my stomach to watch as the baby seal reached the shore and headed right for its dead mother.

I rolled onto my back, hands over my face.

I might as well have hit the baby over the head, because in killing the mother, I'd killed the baby too. And I wept.

## forty-four

Lying on my stomach at the top of the dune, I watched through tears as the baby poked its nose against the dead mother, which was scarcely larger than the baby. That explained why the seal was so skinny. Mother monk seals don't feed at all for the five or six weeks when they nurse their baby, surviving only on their existing blubber. They sometimes lose hundreds of pounds.

I propped up on my elbows.

The baby was beginning to molt, lose black fur in places. So taking into account the baby's size and the state of its fur, it must have been just about ready to be weaned.

Maybe the baby had a chance to survive.

It made a guttural *braaaaap!*

The mother didn't answer.

The baby wanted milk. It nosed around, poking its face into the gash in the mother's side. Then it found one remaining nipple and, with its mother's blood dripping from its whiskers, the baby nursed.

Unable to watch, I trudged back to the raft. Max was asleep or passed out; I couldn't tell anymore. Would he want to eat . . . ? I gagged. *No.* I couldn't.

Later, I went back to check. The mother's body was still there, but the baby was gone. I couldn't bear the thought of the baby coming back to the dead body, again and again, as it lay there decomposing.

And I wanted the body gone so I wouldn't have to look at it and be reminded of what I'd done.

I found my broken board and propped that under the dead seal as a lever, then pushed down on it. The body budged, but barely. So I sat with my back to it, dug my feet into the sand, and pushed.

Nothing.

I was already out of breath, but I knew the mechanics of my lever idea were sound and should work. So I tried again, heaving against the board with all my might. And the body rolled. Slowly but, still, it worked. After another roll, I bent over and leaned my hands on my knees, until I stopped panting.

The mother seal was on a slight incline and after a few more rolls, it went much more easily. Finally, it was at the water's edge.

I was worn-out and couldn't do anymore, so I sat about five feet up the beach and waited for the tide to take over. I watched the on-coming clouds and crossed my fingers they held rain. I was thirsty.

I lay back for just a moment and closed my eye.

Water lapped at my feet and woke me up. It took me a minute to realize where I was. I sat up.

The seal's body was gone.

It was done. Just like that.

The baby would slowly forget its mother ever existed.

Then I heard it.

*Bloop!*

The body popped up about fifteen feet offshore, bobbing there.

Until, with scarcely a splash, the enormous red-and-white open maw of a tiger shark came up out of the water and chomped down. The shark lifted the entire seal out of the water and shook it, like a dog does a toy, before tossing it back in the water. Both disappeared.

My mouth dropped open and my heart pounded. I couldn't breathe.

The shark had to have been close to fifteen feet long, maybe longer.

*Bloop!*

The back half of the seal popped up.

I gasped, on my feet in a second.

And the shark was there again, all teeth and fury. With one bite, the rest of the seal was gone.

My hands clutched at my chest as I tried to catch my breath. One word went around and around in my head; I couldn't even think anything else. Because it was the only word that applied to what I'd just seen.

*Monster.*

## forty-five

Just in case of rain, I spent the next hour or so hunting for water vessels. I found another couple of broken fishing floats and rinsed them out as best as I could without stepping too far into the water. My plan was to never set foot in that water again.

The evening brought rain. At first Max and I sat there open-mouthed, letting the fresh water fill our mouths. It tasted faintly of salt, but it was delicious. "Maybe the rain is my silver parachute."

Max didn't answer.

At least filling my belly with water made me less hungry for a bit. As the rain continued, I stuck some sticks in the sand and hefted the raft on top, creating a pathetic, but dry little shelter to lie under. Well, partly dry. Next time I would know to do it before the rain started, then it would definitely be dry.

I slept for a while and then woke up to darkness, stomach rumbling. Even if I could scrounge up fishing gear, I couldn't fish for anything in the reef. I couldn't risk getting ciguatera. Which didn't leave many options.

In the morning, I was determined to find food.

The small flat field between the raft and the highest dune had obviously been where most of the gooney nests were.

"Ouch!" I'd stepped on something sharp and I looked down. An albatross chick, only a skeleton, still half feathered with silvery black down, most of the body eaten by crabs. I grabbed a stick and probed inside the ribs, what used to be the gullet, poking at a pile of red plastic. Caps from plastic bottles, fake plastic cherries, even a red toy soldier missing one arm.

I shook my head.

One of that season's chicks whose parents had inadvertently killed it. When adult albatross fished on the surface of the ocean, they mainly feasted on squid eggs. But, with all the garbage in the ocean, this chick's parents must have honed in on the color red, and ended up filling their chick's belly with plastic. So it starved to death even though it thought its belly was full. It *had* been full, just full of the wrong stuff.

I kept looking through the nesting ground and saw a large egg. An albatross egg, white with the reddish splotch at the end. Obviously dead. Probably rotten. With my stick, I rolled it over. The bottom was cracked, and the motion split it open.

"Auuuuggghhh!" I covered my nose with my arm, and went running, until I was far enough upwind to not smell it anymore. "Yuck." I shuddered.

I kept moving on my quest. Several sooty terns ran along the ground, chortling at me. They nested on the ground, and I kept my eyes peeled for their speckled little eggs. I found one and squatted beside it. The mother came running along and stood a few feet away.

I was hungry.

The mother looked at her egg, then at me.

My stomach lurched into dry heaves.

I left the egg and the mother and went on my way, finally catching my breath.

As I neared the beach where I'd found the mother seal, I heard barking. The baby. I jogged to the top of the dune and knelt.

The baby seal was there, nosing at a sea cucumber.

Before I saw one, I always thought sea cucumbers were like real cucumbers, some kind of vegetable of the sea. But they were marine creatures, and this one was very dark, close to a foot long, and looked like a big slug. When they felt threatened, their defense was to shoot out strands of sticky stuff, like Silly String. Apparently, this one felt threatened, because the poor seal had tendrils of light greenish goop all over its face and whiskers.

I smiled. Although they were no gourmet feast for a seal, sea cucumbers were plentiful and easy to catch. More than one baby seal has feasted on them before they got good at fishing.

"Way to go, Starbuck."

*Where did that come from?*

For some reason the name just popped out. Maybe too much *Battlestar Galactica* in Honolulu. And a vision of my daily coffee fix. I tried not to think about a latte, whipped cream, caramel.

Maybe I just felt the need to name the seal, make it a companion. And sure, Starbuck was a girl on the TV show, and maybe the baby wasn't. I didn't know. The name just fit.

Starbuck shook her head as she chewed, probably not very happy with all the sticky stuff. As she gnawed, more goop oozed out her mouth and stuck to her snout. She kept working at that sea cucumber until it was gone.

I had a good feeling. She was going to make it.

## forty-six

By the time the third morning on the island came around, at least I think it was the third, I had developed a routine. I woke on the beach, opening my eye to see if anything was different.

My left eye was still swollen shut. Useless.

My nose still hurt so bad I couldn't even sniffle without my eyes tearing up.

My lips were cracked and stung from even the smallest twitch.

I was hungrier than when I'd gone to sleep.

My filthy Bermuda shorts threatened to fall down whenever I stood up, my formerly white camisole was now practically black with dirt and sand and blood, and I was pretty sure my underwear could go for a walk on their own.

Nope, nothing much different with me.

Or with Max, who now slept almost all of the time.

Or with the island.

Shades of the island didn't change.

The sky's bright unbroken blue.

The water's ever-rippling greenish turquoise.

The sand's long stretches of white, interrupted here and there by green plant life and the varied colors of marine debris that floated up every day.

The color scheme had become such an unchanging constant that when I noticed the bright yellow spot in the water, my breath caught in my throat.

I stared, squinted out of my good eye.

The bright yellow was a survival suit, there in the water, just floating.

I stood, watching it get closer until I could see it better. Yellow on top, with a black bottom and attached boots; it looked in good condition.

But the suit wasn't flat.

Was there some sort of compressor inside? Filling it with air? They were no good if they got punctured, I'd read that somewhere, so maybe there was an extra bladder thing inside, keeping it afloat.

My heart pounded, but I didn't want to admit what I was thinking. *Hoping.*

Sometimes those suits had emergency beacons. Maybe this one did. And maybe I could activate it and wait for someone to track it to the island. To me.

I watched it for a bit, but it didn't seem to get any closer to the beach. Despite not wanting to, I entered the water. Wading out to get closer, so I could grab the suit, I hesitated for a moment. The water came up to my ankles, then to my shins.

*Almost there.*

I grabbed one of the black boots and pulled.

"Oh, God."

The suit wasn't empty. I was holding a foot. Which meant—

A wave came then, pushing the weight of the suit at me, and I screamed, trying to shove it away. The suit was full, full of a dead person, full of what was left of whoever that person was. And that person was too heavy for me to push off.

Trying to get away, I stumbled in the water and lost my footing.

Another wave pushed the suit, the body, onto me and I was face-to-face with the eyeless, half-eaten face of a corpse.

Screaming, I shoved, but with the combined action of the wave and the weight of the body, my face ended up pressed against the chest of the suit. Using every ounce of strength I had, I whipped myself around and screamed at a sudden pain in my nose.

Finally, I crawled up onto the beach and cradled my face in my hands, trying to feel the damage. Blood dripped on the sand. The diamond was gone, had gotten caught in something on the suit—maybe the zipper—and ripped out, splitting that side of my nose.

I fell on my side, back to the water, arms wrapped tight around my legs, shuddering and crying.

When I'd finally stopped, I rolled over to face the water.

The survival suit . . . the body . . . was still there in the shallows, the waves pushing it onto the beach, but never far enough to stay for long. Eventually, the motion of the waves pulled it back, moving it away from me.

I stood up.

Max spoke to me then. He hadn't spoken in a long time.

For days, it seemed.

He said, "You need that suit. You need that beacon."

I shook my head. "No." I sniffled, which hurt like hell. "I'm not going back out there!" My voice had lost any semblance of calm, and everything that came out of my mouth was high-pitched and child-like and uncontrolled. "I'm not."

He kept telling me to go, go get the suit. If I stood any chance of getting it, I would have to go in the next minute or two. Get back in that water.

Max didn't leave me alone. "Get in there and get it. You have to."

"No!" I screamed. "No, I don't!" I flung myself onto the wet sand and lay there.

I didn't have to do anything.

I just had to lie there. Lie there and bleed to death.

Lie there and die.

I didn't care. I didn't have to do anything.

I didn't.

## forty-seven

My left cheek lay on the cool, wet sand. With my good eye, I watched the yellow suit.

*There might not even be a beacon on the suit.*

*If there is, someone would have found it by now.*

*Or the thing is broken.*

I gave myself more excuses to not go in that water.

And Max said, "You have to."

Closing my eye, I said, "Shut up." And I couldn't stop. "Shut up! Shut up! Shut up!"

And then I sat up and screamed, screamed until my head hurt and I had almost no voice left. And then I stood up, turned toward Max, and used what voice I had left to say what I hadn't been able to.

"You're not real! You're dead! You were dead when I shoved you out of the raft." I was panting and had to pause to catch my breath. "I made you up because I couldn't stand to think about what I'd done to save myself." I pointed at him. "I brought you back so I wouldn't have to be alone . . ."

Hearing the truth out loud made me gasp and cover my mouth.

The admission that I was just talking to myself, had been since the second day on the raft, was too much to take. I dropped to my knees, curling my body up and covering my ears with my hands.

I didn't want to hear whatever else I might say out loud. Saying it out loud made it true. And truth was brutal.

The real Max hadn't said a word since the first night. Since he saved my life, twice, and I was ungrateful and yelled at him. He hadn't said anything since I'd asked him if there was anything worse and he said, "Yes."

*Yes.*

That was the last word he ever said because he never woke up.

"He never woke up."

I shook my head.

"Shut up."

The rest was all my imagination. Every conversation. It was just me.

I rocked back and forth. "Shut up."

It was all me trying to stay sane.

First I shoved his body overboard to save my own life. Then I used him, the memory of him, what little I knew of him, to stay alive.

And when I couldn't do it anymore, when I needed something from him, when I needed him to talk to me, I read his journal. I read his journal and pretended it was him talking to me, telling me his story. And I didn't even know how it ended, would never know, because I'd lost the ditty bag when I came over the reef.

Max probably never even knew my name. He died in the raft with a strange, selfish girl who shoved his body overboard to save herself.

And the truth was I only had myself. The entire time I only had myself.

And where had it gotten me?

I was a starving, thirsty, bleeding mess with one good eye.

There was no one to make me go in that water except myself. And I was too much of a coward. Not brave enough to save myself.

Not brave enough.

Or was I?

# forty-eight

Tears blurred my vision and I sobbed so hard my stomach hurt. I wiped my eyes, wincing at the pain when I touched my left one. I sat up.

The yellow suit was still out there, about fifty yards offshore.

I took a deep breath, which came out a racking shudder.

Getting to my feet, I waded into the water, leading with my right side so I could see. I kept going. To my ankles, then my shins, my knees, and my waist. The suit was still a ways off. I looked down at the water.

A drop of blood fell from my nose, just a momentary dark spot in the water before it dispersed and disappeared. Another did the same before I pulled up my shirt and held it to my nose.

With a tentative step, then pause . . . step, then pause . . . I kept going.

By the time the water reached my chest, I was almost to the suit.

I sensed something to my left and had to turn my whole head to see that side.

Nothing.

But the word popped into my head.

*Monster.*

"Stop it."

Keeping time with my quick, shallow breaths, my heart pulsed in my ears.

*Whoosh whoosh whoosh.*

The suit was a mere step away.

*Whoosh whoosh whoosh.*

But the water was a little cloudy out there. I couldn't tell, for sure, if the depth was the same. But I only had to move a little bit, not even a whole step.

I clenched my fists.

*Whoosh whoosh whoosh.*

The suit could mean rescue. Salvation. Getting off this stupid island.

I went for it.

The bottom dropped out, and I sank, kicking until I came up sputtering. Lashing out, I hit the suit with a hand. Jerking back at first, I realized it would keep me up. With a hand, I grabbed ahold, and the buoyancy helped me right myself. I took a firmer grip of the arm, trying not to think about what I was holding, and starting kicking for shore.

Again, I sensed something, but this time it was my right side.

Nothing.

Again, the word popped into my head.

*Monster.*

The waves helped my progress until I was able to touch the bottom and walk again, and I breathed a sigh of relief when the water was finally just a bit above my waist.

"Almost there."

With one hand I dragged the suit behind me as I walked, fighting the waves.

Then suddenly, I was tugged backward and lost my hold on the suit. I turned my back to the shore to grab it again, but the suit was gone. Nowhere in sight.

I froze and stopped breathing.

*Bloop!*

About five yards away, farther out from the shore, a black boot from the suit popped up. The top of it spun toward me, revealing torn flesh and white pointy shards of bone.

Adrenaline exploded, and the resulting heat flushed through my body as my banging heart felt like it would erupt out my ears.

A dark shadow appeared underwater. The tiger shark surfaced and took the boot in one gulp.

And I couldn't think for the sound, the sound that wouldn't stop. The sound hurt, hurt my ears and my head and my brain.

Screaming.

The sound was me and I couldn't stop it.

*Move!* Max. Max was telling me to move.

No, there was no Max. Not anymore. It was just me. Me telling myself to move.

*Robie, you have to move.* But I couldn't.

And then I turned toward shore. Max stood at the water's edge, frantically beckoning to me.

*Robie, if you don't move, you will die.*

And I did. Move that is, not die. But any moment—

*Monster . . .*

And I was running . . .

*Grab me . . .*

splashing . . .

*Bite me . . .*

crawling . . .

*Pull me back in . . .*

scrambling . . .

*Chomp me in half like the seal . . .*

My screams, though becoming ragged, were still so loud they nearly drowned out the heartbeat pounding in my ears.

On the beach, Max still beckoned to me as I clawed my way through the water and didn't stop fighting. Or screaming.

Not even when I reached the sand, dragged myself up away from the water, and collapsed in a shivering heap at his feet.

Pushing myself up, I looked back at the water.

The shark was still there, a dark shadow circling where the suit had been. Looking for more of a meal.

"You monster!" I yelled. "Monster!" My words were choking sobs. "You can't have me! You can't have me . . ."

And the shadow came closer to shore, so much closer than I ever imagined a shark of that size could come.

Was anywhere safe?

I screamed again, but the scream morphed into a wail and then faded to weak whimpers as I dropped back down and curled myself up in a ball, a wet and shaking ball, as I rocked back and forth.

Max wasn't real. He had never woken up. And I had pushed him off the raft.

I wished I hadn't admitted that to myself. Because I needed him then. I needed him. I couldn't do it alone.

So I brought him back.

"I'm here," he said. He sat beside me and took my head in his lap.

I just needed a few moments of comfort.

Just a few moments.

Then I would let him go.

## forty—nine

I didn't expect Max to be there when I opened my eye.

He wasn't real. I was more than aware I'd made him up. I'd made him up to help myself.

I wasn't insane though. At least I didn't think so.

I would save him for when I really needed someone. I would ration him.

The shadow in the water was gone. The monster had vanished.

I breathed out.

Vowing to never step foot in the lagoon again, I stood and went to check if my containers had anything left. One of them had enough so I could have a long drink of the tepid, stale water. I choked it down and tapped the bottom to get every last drop.

The water was gone.

I needed to move and trudged toward the other side of the island. Starbuck was sleeping in the sun when I rounded the corner. I dropped to the sand about ten feet away from her and just lay there, still breathing hard.

I whispered, "I almost died. I almost got eaten by a shark."

Her eyes stayed closed.

I spoke normally, "Starbuck, did you hear what just happened?"

I shook my head. "I'm talking to a seal." Worse than that, I was waiting for her to answer.

And then I felt something bubble up inside. Not more of the sobs that had fueled the tears that had recently dried salty on my cheeks. I couldn't hold back as the laughter exploded, so long and hard I found myself holding my stomach because it hurt. "Oh, my God . . ." I tried to catch my breath. "I almost got eaten by a shark . . ." And I laughed some more, until my lips stung and the tears flowed freely and I couldn't even breathe.

I rolled on my back and just looked up at the blue sky, shielding my eyes from the sun with one hand as I let the laughter disperse at last.

Had I lost it? Maybe I *had* gone insane.

Or maybe I was so on edge that my emotions were all boiling up, getting mixed and gnarled, leaving me with no control over which one would show up next. Or maybe I'd just run out of fear and grief.

Laughter was all that was left.

So, taking a deep breath, I let it out.

When the last guffaw finally faded, I found myself spent, but relaxed, calm even.

Crazy.

A giggle popped out before I could stop it.

Yeah. I was definitely losing it.

I lay there for a while, napping in the sun along with Starbuck. She was definitely skinnier than the first time I saw her. I imagined going cold turkey on her rich diet of mother's milk had been a shock to the system. Sea cucumbers and algae were a weak substitute.

I wished I could help, but I couldn't even feed myself.

The sun was too hot on my skin and I headed slowly back to the raft.

I thought of all the food I'd eaten in my life. All the food I'd *wasted* in my life. That Happy Meal in Honolulu that ended up on the ground. I didn't even care then, not really. There was always more food. Always.

Not anymore.

There was a lump in my throat. I swallowed to get rid of it, but it stayed.

All the meals my mom made me. My favorites. Her French toast. She dunked day-old bread in a mixture of beaten eggs and vanilla, fried the slices in butter, then sifted powdered sugar on top before drizzling hot maple syrup over the stack.

My chin quivered involuntarily.

Mom's weird pizza. She made whole wheat dough in the bread maker, let it rise, then rolled it out and slathered it with barbecue sauce, chunks of bacon, grilled chicken, cheese, and some drips of ranch dressing.

Tears welled up in my right eye and spilled down my cheek.

I wiped them away with the back of my hand and sighed. I reached the raft and pulled it over me, anything to get out of the brutal sun.

*Clack! Clack! Clack!*

One of the few remaining albatross chicks stood a few feet away, warning me not to get too close. I couldn't really tell, but he seemed like a male to me. "Hey, you walked over to me, buddy."

*Clack! Clack!*

"You should fly away. There's nothing left here for you."

If he didn't leave soon, he would die here. Like all the other carcasses scattered around the island. I tried to imagine his dilemma. Do you wait for your parents to show up one last time with food? And if you do wait, how long? Hunger is a powerful feeling that has been sending albatross chicks on their first journey since forever. But wait one day too many and you'll be too weak to fly.

I could empathize with that.

"How long since *you* ate?"

His dark eyes sparkled, and the brilliant black under them made him look wise. His new adult feathers ruffled in the wind, the last bit of silvery baby fluff barely clinging to the top of his snow-white head. He spread his wings, catching the breeze and floating a few feet off the ground before landing again with another *clack*!

"See? You know how to fly. You have to go." I nodded. "You have to go."

And maybe he heard me, maybe he understood, because with one shrill call to the sky, he spread his wings, caught the wind, and deftly flapped his way out above the lagoon.

I applauded. "Go, dude. Go."

About fifty yards out, he slowed and began to drop.

"No! Keep going!"

He plopped into the water.

"Fold your wings! Fold your wings!"

He floated there, wings held out straight.

I groaned. "Fold your wings. You have to fold your wings."

But instead, he held them out to the sides until they began to droop. Once the tips touched the water, he struggled to get them to flap. But they wouldn't, because they were too soaked and heavy.

I covered my face with my hands.

He couldn't fly. So he would float there, until either a shark found him or he just succumbed.

Doomed. He was doomed.

Maybe he wasn't the only one.


The sun was about to set on another day without food. I'd gone back to the spot where I saw the sooty tern egg, but found that it had hatched into a tiny fuzz ball. I'd searched for more, but realized it was too late in the season, and that chick might not even have much of a chance.

There were a handful of albatross chicks left on the island, along with some other birds, but that was pretty much it. Well, not to mention me and Starbuck, if you wanted to count all living things.

I sighed.

*Barely* living.

I knew I could go a long time without food. But not water. I pinched the skin on the back of my hand and it was slow to return.

"It better rain soon."

I watched the sun turn almost tangerine as it neared the horizon. Just as it slipped below, for a split second, a shimmering ray of green appeared on the water.

I squealed. "A green flash!"

How many sunsets on Midway had I sat on the beach in front of the Clipper House, hoping to see a green flash? So many people off boats had told me about seeing one, and I never had.

"About time!"

Sailors long held that a green flash meant good weather, and I'd memorized an English saying. I smiled and said the words aloud:

"Glimpse you ere the green ray, count the morrow a fine day."

As I listened to myself, I stopped smiling. Because the last thing I needed was for the morrow, for any of my morrows, to be fine.

Because what I really needed was rain.

## fifty

After another night, I walked slowly along the beach as the sun rose on another cloudless day. I needed to get off the island, and if someone else wasn't going to do it for me, I would. I walked over to the highest dune; the pile of wood still lay where it had rolled down. I started piling it up, constructing a signal fire.

When I had a good pile, I tucked in some dried grasses from gooney nests as tinder. One spark, and if all went well, the pile would burst into flame. I spent quite a while testing each cigarette lighter I'd gathered. When I didn't get a spark, I broke the top off with a rock, and poured any lighter fluid into an empty plastic Pepsi bottle that was too moldy and gross for me to use for drinking water. For now, at least.

By afternoon, I had about a half inch of lighter fluid in the bottom. I sighed.

For so much work, the return seemed so little. Still, I climbed back up the dune and set the bottle in a secure spot. Ready. I was ready. If I ever found a lighter that worked. Or lightning struck my pile.

It was all a long shot, I knew that. But at least I was doing something.

After a nap under the raft, to get out of the sun, I resumed my beachcombing.

Something red caught my eye and I walked toward it, then began jogging. Immediately, my vision began to swim and I stopped, dropped my head down, and rested my hands on my knees. I rested there a moment until I caught my breath, then walked slowly over to the object.

I poked it with my toe and grinned.

Santa Claus. *My* Santa Claus.

I picked him up.

When I went over the reef in the raft, he'd been in it. He made it ashore. But did anything else?

What would be the most useful thing from the raft?

If I could only pick one, I'd pick the Coastal Commander with the flares. And the mirror. I could start a fire with one, couldn't I?

Yeah, the mirror would be great.

As I kept beachcombing, I wondered how long Santa had been there. Had I missed things among all the marine debris?

The only thing to do was keep looking, and I focused on the area where I found Santa. New garbage seemed to pile up every few hours. A glint of something caught my eye.

"Whoa." Forest-green glass, about the size of a basketball, the fishing float was encased in light green fishing net and barnacles. I picked it up, straining because it was heavy. Well, heavy for me, since I was so weak. The glass ball stunk of rotten fish and mildew.

As I shifted to get a better grip, a stream of water rolled around the inside.

Bending at the waist, I set the ball down and rolled it slowly, looking for leaks. There were none. The water was on the inside. The ball had gone to depths so deep that the water pressure forced water through the glass. I smiled. I'd seen only one intact glass ball like that before, and it was a lot smaller than this one.

As I picked it up again, heading back to the raft, my foot brushed against something yielding and soft. Something that didn't feel like the usual marine debris.

I closed my eye for a second. "Please let it be the Coastal Commander."

The Coastal Commander wasn't there. But something else was.

I dropped the ball gently into the sand and knelt beside Max's ditty bag.

I pulled it into my lap, unbuckled it, then unzipped it. Everything was as I'd left it. The manifest. The Survival at Sea card. And Max's journal.

Maybe he wasn't done talking to me yet.

# Max

*That summer, after graduation, I bought Taylor Swift tickets. Brandy was so excited. The only hitch was getting her mom to let her go with me. Almost to Boise, over a two-hour drive. A hotel was not even an option.*

*It took a lot of convincing, but Brandy talked her mom into it. She couldn't stop grinning as she climbed into my blue pickup. Her dark hair was loose and long. She'd curled it on the ends. Her dress was flowery, cowboy boots on her feet. She teased me about my outfit, which was my standard: jeans, wrestling tournament T-shirt, and Nikes. I said, "No one will look at me when I'm standing next to you anyway."*

*She kissed me on the cheek.*

*On the drive over, Brandy made me listen to every Taylor Swift song on her iPod. Not my favorite, but I sang along with Brandy, even though I couldn't sing. She made me so happy. I would do about anything to make her happy.*

*The drive took forever. Construction. Lane closed. I was worried we'd be late. But we were plenty early to the concert, which was crazy with people. The concert was a blur. A loud blur. My ears rang when we stepped outside in the dark. I remember Brandy laughing. The moment was almost in slow motion. One of those moments that seems to last forever. Like when I lost in state finals that year.*

*Things just slowed down. And I don't know why, but I shivered.*

## fifty-one

I swallowed and set the notebook down. My one eye was shot. I'd have to save the rest for later.

I pulled the other things out of the bag and set them on the sand. Fantasizing about the chance of a wayward Skittle, I ran my hand inside. There was a lump.

Peering inside, it was clear the bag was empty. I stuck my hand back in and felt around. I turned the bag inside out and noticed a small rip in the lining. I ran my fingers along it and followed the lump, then stuck a finger in and, with the tip of it, felt something solid.

I held my breath for a moment.

And then I let it out, told myself not to get my hopes up. The chance of there being anything in there of any consequence, of any help to me at all, was ridiculously small.

Even while I was telling myself this, I knew I would rip the lining to get at whatever it was. Because I still had hope. Dwindling, but still there.

I gently tore the lining until I could reach in. I felt something hard, about three inches long, and then, as I pulled it out, I saw the red top and yellow tube. My face crumpled as I couldn't hold back the tears.

*At last. At last.*

*My silver parachute.*

Carmex. A roll-up tube of Carmex.

I kissed it and cradled it to my chest for a moment, thanking Max, thanking God, thanking whoever put that ditty bag on the beach. And then, with a snap, I popped off the cap and inhaled the camphor and menthol, then smeared the warm salve on my lips.

My smile stretched out my lips so far I had to apply Carmex again, just to cover them. The relief was soothing and immediate and I couldn't stop smiling.

With a finger, I took some and dotted it onto my nose. I couldn't believe it was possible that I'd ever missed the Carmex in the first place. But it had to have been there all along. Right?

Making sure I hadn't gotten any sand in the tube, I closed the Carmex and shoved it deep in my pocket, then returned everything else to the bag and set it on the raft.

My excitement over the find gave me a little burst of energy. I walked a little ways down the beach before the burst waned and I plopped down in the sand to rest. Some lighters were within my reach, and I used a washed-up stick to drag some others close enough for me to grab them. I had found several when one caught my eye. At first, I didn't even know it was a lighter, because it wasn't like the others, it was decorated with a portrait of Marilyn Monroe. I stuck it in my pocket with the Carmex. When I felt rested, I stood up and kept walking.

As I rounded the beach where I'd washed up, I saw one albatross standing on the bank. She flapped her wings, caught a little air, and then landed again.

"You'd better go or you won't make it."

Not wanting to watch another one die, I kept walking. My stomach rumbled. And I turned back. She clacked her bill, but made no move to fly.

She was going to die, plain and simple. And if I didn't eat soon, I would probably die too.

The Survival at Sea adage flashed in my head: **Eat any bird you can catch.**

She was going to die anyway.

I took a slow step back toward her.

Could I catch her?

I took another slow step and she just looked at me.

I could try.

With a burst of energy I didn't know I had, I leaped up the bank toward her, but with a rush of flapping wings, she flew over my head, out to sea.

I whipped around, disappointed at first, but then I watched her go. She flew about fifty yards, landing exactly where the other one had landed.

"Fold your wings!" I yelled. "Fold your—"

Very neatly, she tucked in her wings and sat there, floating.

"Wings . . ."

So she'd passed the first test.

She sat there for a while.

And then I saw a fin and groaned. The albatross was toast.

"Go!" I screamed.

She began to run on the water and flap her wings.

"Faster! Flap faster!"

The fin was nearly to the albatross, and the monster's head burst out of the water and snapped, just as the gooney lifted off, flying again.

Lifting both arms in the air, I shouted, "Yes!"

And she flapped until she was gone from view.

Dropping to my butt in the sand, I sighed.

Maybe not everything on this island was doomed.

Maybe just I was.

# fifty-two

I found a bunch more lighters and took them up to my signal fire. I tried each one before breaking them and sprinkling their fluid on the tinder.

I heard Starbuck growling. As I topped the dune, I saw her in the water, just at the edge of the beach. I ran toward her, stopping just far enough way so I wouldn't startle her.

"Oh, no . . ."

She was wrapped up in light blue plastic fishing net. I hated to get any nearer and scare her, but on closer inspection, she was wrapped up in a whole network of the net, like she'd swam right into a pile of marine debris and become ensnared.

One flipper was free and she pushed with it, trying to get up on the sand, but it wasn't enough to move her.

I wanted to help so badly, but didn't know how.

*Not again.*

I sat down and watched her struggle. She was a little bit farther out in the water, but not making any progress toward getting untangled.

Maybe I could go behind her, where she couldn't see me, and try to get some of the net loose.

*You'll have to go in the water.*

I waited until she was looking away from me and then ran down into the water, just up to my knees, trying not to splash. I kept looking behind me for shadows under the surface.

The net was so tight that I could barely slip my hand between it and her back flipper. As soon as I touched her, she flinched and tried to turn her head to see me, but she was so entangled, she couldn't. She must have started struggling immediately when she got caught, which just made the net wrap tighter around her.

I gave up on the flipper and went to her back end. The net there was even tighter, and I couldn't get even a finger in.

She was still struggling, trying to get up the beach. I needed something to cut the net off.

I splashed back through the water toward the raft, but had to stop halfway to sit down and catch my breath before finally reaching it. There was a big pile of marine debris near the raft, and I'd only looked for lighters. Maybe I'd find something sharp. Sharp enough to cut the net.

With a stick, I dug through. I pushed over a board and stopped. I wiped the sweat off my forehead and bent down. With two fingers, I plucked out what looked like a knife.

It was just a piece of rusted metal, wickedly jagged on one side, but it looked like it would cut. There wasn't any other option, so I got a safer grip on it and headed back for Starbuck.

She was a little farther out in the water. Ignoring her cries of warning, I splashed around behind her and slipped my knife in between the net and her flipper and started sawing, careful not to cut her. Luckily, she was so tangled that she couldn't get her head close enough to bite me.

The plastic was tough, but I managed to cut one piece off. The work was draining, and I had to stop and wipe my forehead off and catch my breath. Finally, I had her flipper loose.

But the rest of her was still hopelessly tangled, and now, in addition to trying to get herself loose, she was trying to get away from me.

In as soothing a tone as I could muster, I said, "I'm trying to help you. I'm trying to help you."

In spite of her very vocal protests, I moved around to her side, putting myself between her and the beach, and started sawing at the net on her back. And then she stopped making noise. And splashing.

I stopped what I was doing and stepped back so I could see all of her with my one eye.

Her head sagged in the water.

The light blue plastic had become a noose around her neck, strangling her, and my loosening the back had only made it possible for the net to tighten more around her neck as she struggled.

"No!"

I pushed on her. "Starbuck!"

She didn't move.

She was gone.

I stepped back until my feet hit the beach, then dropped to my knees. "Not again. Not again. Not again!" I threw the knife off to the side.

The waves gently pushed her up onshore.

I was the only one left.

My empty stomach cramped. And an absolutely unthinkable idea made its way into my head.

I shook my head. No, I wouldn't do it.

To get rid of the thought, I got up and ran, ran away from Starbuck, dead on the beach. I ran, ran back to the raft, where I threw myself down on the sand.

I was dizzy and could barely breathe, and I lay there until my heart stopped pounding.

My lips were dry again. I reached into my pocket for the Carmex and instead, my fingers curled around something else. I pulled out the Marilyn Monroe lighter.

More out of habit than hope, I flicked the wheel with my thumb.

A spark sputtered.

I nearly dropped the lighter at first, but managed to hold on. Afraid it wouldn't light up again, I held my breath as I flicked the wheel once more.

Another slight hint of a spark.

I exhaled. "Please please please." I looked up at the sky. "Third time's the charm, right?" My hand trembled, so I gripped my wrist with my other hand to steady it.

"Come on."

My thumb slid the wheel and a flame popped up, wavering, but steady. I held it for a moment, then let it go out.

Lifting the lighter to my lips, I kissed Marilyn Monroe.

I had fire. *I had fire.*

# fifty-three

Suddenly, my unthinkable idea by the beach didn't seem so unthinkable. If I was going to save myself, I had to think selfishly. I'd already proved that—hadn't I?—when I'd put Max in the water to save myself. But he had been gone. I hadn't killed him. A fine line, yes, but one I had to live with if I was going to . . . well . . . live.

Starbuck was gone. I wouldn't let the monster take her. I needed her more.

Maybe I wasn't worth the saving. Maybe my life wasn't worth Max's. Maybe my life wasn't worth Starbuck's. But if it wasn't, why was I still alive?

Their deaths would be worth nothing, mean nothing, if I didn't make it. Max had saved me. He gave me a chance to live. And if I didn't take that chance and run with it . . .

I walked to the bank and looked out over the water, thinking. Something caught my eye down the beach.

A huge green sea turtle, nearly the size of a table top, had crawled up on the beach and lay there, sunning itself.

My gaze went to the henna turtle on my ankle. I bent over and traced it with my hand. The tattoo was in terrific shape, the one part of me that was actually not any worse for wear. My aumakua.

The sea turtle lay there, content.

A sign?

I shrugged. Maybe. It was whatever I wanted it to be.

Back at the raft, I put the Carmex and the lighter in Max's ditty bag, then put the cord around my arm. The trip to the beach took a while. I had to stop three times to rest. Once there, I found my make-shift knife and stood over Starbuck, my heart pounding.

I shook my head.

*Not Starbuck. Not anymore.*

I wanted to apologize. Instead, I started to cry and said, "I want to live. I just want to live. You get that, don't you?"

And I sawed off a piece of meat, stuck it on the end of my knife, and started to carry it back to my signal fire.

I got dizzy and stopped, leaning over to put a hand on my knee and take a break. "No rush."

I looked at the top of the dune. Had it always been that far away?

I had to stop again before I reached the base of the dune, and then had to drop to all fours and crawl up.

Kneeling beside the signal fire, I held the lighter out. "Please work. Please, please work."

I cupped my hand around the dry grass, flicked the wheel, and the tinder sparked. A little breeze blew through, igniting the fire, and soon my pile was ablaze, the smoke invading my sinuses. But I didn't turn my head. The smell was so welcome.

I couldn't cheer. I didn't have anything left to cheer with.

The fire grew quickly.

I set the ditty bag to the side and sat there, watching the fire. Then I stood and held the heaviness at the end of the knife over the flame.

The flesh sizzled in the flame. I pictured myself chewing it, swallowing.

And then I let it drop.

"Max?"

He was there and I laid my head in his lap and gazed at the fire.

"I don't want to live that much," I told him. "Not that much."

Together we watched the fire build and build, until the flames went high and the smoke went up into the clear blue sky.

And he told me more.

# Max

We were about halfway into the drive home, Taylor Swift blaring, of course, when Brandy fell asleep on my shoulder. I was going through the curvy part of the drive and Brandy kept slipping off. She looked so uncomfortable, so I nudged her, and told her to move over by the window and use my jacket for a pillow.

Her seat belt clicked open as I turned back to the road and saw an antelope in my headlights.

I tried to swerve as I braked. But I slammed into the antelope. We went into a skid, headed for the closed construction lane. The tires squealed and Brandy screamed. I put out a hand to protect her just as I lost control. The windshield shattered. We rolled.

The top of the truck was the bottom and then the top again as metal crunched. I don't know if I yelled. I don't remember.

We stopped then, halfway rolled over. The truck teetering back one more time, its top on the ground. The engine had stopped. Taylor Swift was still singing and the dashboard lights were still on. I smelled gas. And heard water.

Hanging upside down by my seat belt, I reached down and felt water. We were upside down in a creek.

She didn't answer. I reached out to touch her. I couldn't feel her. My head was stuck, so I couldn't look. I reached up and undid my seat belt. I fell to the ceiling and rolled her way, trying to keep my head above the rising water.

Brandy wasn't there.

I crawled out what remained of the windshield. Later, I was in a lot of pain, but right then I screamed her name over and over. I moved away from the truck, knee-deep in water, and made it to the road.

Brandy lay where she'd been thrown through the windshield as soon as we'd rolled, just off the road.

I ran to her, flung myself down beside her. Yelled her name.

Oh, God.

Her neck was at an impossible angle and I held her hand to my chest.

I yelled for help. We were in the middle of nowhere. We'd passed one car in the last hour. I felt in my pocket for my cell phone. My hands were shaking so bad I could barely push the numbers. I waited for 911 to pick up.

A woman's voice. She kept asking questions. I kept answering.

We were a long way out. She was sending help, but it would be a long time. Too long. She told me to hang on.

Brandy didn't move.

I already knew. Still, I held my head to her chest. No heartbeat.

I already knew. Still, I held a hand in front of her mouth and nose. No breath.

With a hand, I touched her cheek. Warm and sticky.

I held her to my chest and started to rock as I sobbed, my face in her hair, smelling her. How could she be gone if she still smelled so good? I straightened her hair, pushing it back over her shoulders like she liked it. It was so soft. So soft.

I heard a sound.

The antelope I'd hit lay in the road, about ten yards away from *me. Another, this one with horns, stood over it, looking down. Then he looked at me as I lay in the road, holding my dead girlfriend.*

*The mountain night was cold enough that his breath was a puff as it came out his nostrils. He was motionless, staring at me.*

*He didn't need me to tell him not to love. Ever.*

# fifty-four

I said, "I'm sorry, Max," and started to cry. But when I reached up to wipe away my tears, there were none. My face was dry.

There were a few pages left, but I was so tired, I couldn't see straight anymore. I lay down on my side and fell asleep.

When I woke up, I was still tired. So tired.

My throat was so dry, I could barely swallow.

I rolled on my back and looked up at the sky. Cloudless. Again.

That color blue used to be my favorite. I'd grown to hate it.

What was the last thing I'd had to drink?

Days before, the last water from my makeshift bowl.

When had I last felt the urge to pee?

I couldn't even remember.

I licked my lips. So parched. I pulled out the Carmex and covered them.

All I could do was watch the smoke spiral in the breeze.

Max said, "You can't let the fire go out."

I looked at the small pile of wood only steps away. "I'm too tired."

"You have to."

I got to my hands and knees and crawled over to the pile. I grabbed a piece in each hand and crawled back, then tossed them into the fire, which quickly renewed itself.

I collapsed on my back again, staring at the blue above me.

*If I get out of this . . .*

"I will . . ."

*What?*

*I will be happy with my life. I will feel lucky, because I am. I am lucky, just to have a house and food and water and parents who love me . . .*

"But I don't have any of those things."

*I'm not lucky at all. Not anymore.*

My face crumpled and I sobbed invisible tears. Invisible tears that were a sign.

I covered my face with my arms. "I'm not gonna make it. I'm not."

Would my parents ever know what happened to me?

Would *anyone*?

I rolled on my side. An albatross skeleton lay not far from me, feathers still clinging to the bone. Maybe I would end up like that. Maybe it would be years before anyone stumbled across my body. Maybe, when someone did find me, they wouldn't even be able to tell who I was.

I put my hands together, praying.

Was I? Not really. When I was little I did say my prayers every night. But when it was just me, and I was older, without Mom and Dad putting me to bed, I stopped.

Midway didn't even have a church. We did have a white cross though, on an edge of the island, overlooking the lagoon. A metal plaque on it said something about the cross being 140 miles from the international dateline and that, traditionally, the world's last Easter sunrise service was held there every year.

Every Easter, the residents of Midway did gather at the cross at sunrise. Sometimes someone read from the Bible or said a few words. Usually we sang a hymn.

This year I had slept in.

I slipped my hands under my head and shut my eye.

I could bargain with God. Isn't that what people did in these situations?

"Dear God . . ." I stopped.

Somehow praying now, when I really needed something, seemed too little too late. Besides, if God was up there, He could make His own decisions. Truth was, I had no strength to plead my case.

I hoped sleep would find me fast.

## fifty–five

My dreams were of cats. Spitting. Then snakes. Hissing.

The spitting and hissing seemed so real.

My face almost felt wet.

My eye opened. My face *was* wet.

The sky was cloudy and there was *rain*.

I sat up and put my open mouth to the sky. Just drips, barely enough to dampen my lips.

After a while, my neck cramped and I looked back down.

Steam. There was steam coming from my fire.

"No!" I lunged forward and grabbed the end of a stick from the fire. I started pushing the charred wood around. "Come on, come on." But there were no more flames, and the wood was all wet.

I looked back up at the sky, at the dark clouds moving off to the east.

How had I missed the rain?

My hair was damp. I stuck some of it in my mouth and sucked, trying to get out any moisture I could. I felt my camisole. Damp as well. Frantic, I yanked it over my head and twisted it, trying to wring whatever was there into my open mouth.

Not enough. Not enough.

I hugged myself and cried more dry tears. There had been rain, enough to put my fire out. But not enough for me to get a drink.

I didn't bother to put my top back on and just fell to my side.

My face smashed in the sand as I watched the last bit of steam rise from the fire.

The signal fire. The fire that was supposed to save my life.

Suddenly, I felt a chill. I put my top back on and looked around for my hoodie. My gaze drifted to the horizon.

Then I gasped.

A white ship with blue writing, right in front of me.

*Was it really there? Was it just a mirage?*

*A hallucination brought on by dehydration?*

I froze. If it was a hallucination, I would die. Die from disappointment.

So I told myself it wasn't real. And I sat and waited to see if I was right.

## fifty–six

My imaginary ship didn't move, just sat there. Anchored out at sea. I couldn't read the blue letters, but had seen enough to know it was a NOAA ship.

I knew what NOAA stood for. National Oceanographic and . . . something . . .

I tapped my forehead. "You know this." I couldn't even think straight. Funny, that my imaginary ship would be a NOAA one. Coast Guard would have made more sense though. For a rescuer.

I sat up straight.

Coast Guard would have made much more sense. And wouldn't a hallucination make sense? I mean, it would be a fantasy, right? Something I would want to see. Like Coast Guard. NOAA was just dumb.

There on the top of the dune, I hugged my knees and watched. A boat lowered into the water. And came toward the island.

*It's a hallucination.*

Max stood at the bottom of the dune and looked up at me. "It's not a hallucination."

I told him, "But that's all you are."

The boat got closer. *Say it was real, just say it was.* Had they seen my fire?

The boat neared the beach on the farthest point of the island from me. Wouldn't a hallucination have them land closer, be more convenient? Two people hopped out and pulled the boat onto the beach and more people got out. They just stood around.

If it was my hallucination, wouldn't they come right for me?

Maybe they *were* real.

I stood up. My legs collapsed beneath me and I rolled down the dune, landing at the bottom by Max. I could no longer see the boat or the people.

Because they weren't there.

I laid my head on my arms, not wanting to get around the dune. Not wanting to look out at the sea. Not wanting to see . . . nothing.

If that's all it was, a hallucination, why exert myself? I was done.

"But it's not a hallucination." Max crouched in front of me. "Robie, you have to do this. You have to get to the beach." He backed up slightly. "Come on. Come with me."

I shook my head. "I can't."

He nearly shouted at me. "You can. You can."

I got up on all fours and crawled a few feet, then fell forward onto my face. "I can't."

"Get up!" He backed up, beckoning to me.

Up on my knees again, I followed him until I was nearly around the dune.

Walking ahead a bit, he turned to me. "Just a little farther. You can do this."

I looked up at him. "Are you saving me again?"

"No." He shook his head. "This is all you."

Grunting, I put my head down and crawled, crawled until I had nothing left, and then I fell onto my side. I looked up and saw the boat. It was still there. So were the people.

I tried to scream. I didn't even have any words, just screeches.

I tried to get to my knees, but fell down. So I rolled over on my back, raised my arms in the air, and kept screaming until there was nothing left. I shut my eye.

*Please let the ship be real.*

I wasn't sure how much later it was when I heard arguing.

A woman's voice. "We have to get her to the ship."

"I'm not sure we should move her." A man.

"She might die if we don't." The woman again.

Another man said, "What the hell is she doing out here?"

I opened my eyes to two faces peering down at me. One was a woman with kind green eyes and curly red hair, the other a guy in a blue ball cap and a salt-and-pepper beard. They both wore blue shirts with NOAA on them.

I couldn't do anything but blink. *Are they real?*

The guy said, "She's awake." He smiled and touched my arm. "You're gonna be okay." He helped me sit up and he and the woman held me up. Then they put a bottle of water to my lips. With both hands, I held it and gulped so fast that more of it ran down my chin than went into my mouth.

There was no way that water was a hallucination, because I'd never tasted any so cold and clear and delicious in my entire frickin' life.

I chugged that bottle so fast that my temples ached. I scrunched my eyes and pressed my palms into my forehead.

The guy in the cap said, "I'm Brian. We're with NOAA."

He talked so slow. Did he think I was dumb or something?

"You saw my fire."

He looked over at the woman and shook his head. "No. We're on a research trip and wanted to check out the island." He shrugged. "We almost didn't stop."

They hadn't seen my fire. They just happened to show up. On my island.

The woman asked my name.

Even after all that water, my voice sounded raspy. "Robie."

"Well, Robie, let's get you to the ship, okay?"

I nodded. "But Max—"

The woman's forehead wrinkled. "Someone else is here?"

I started to say something, then got a grip. I bit my lip and shook my head. "No. No one else. "

Another guy came up. His eyes were brown and kind and crinkled around the edges when he smiled. "I'll carry you over to the boat." He gently put one arm around me and the other under my legs, picking me up.

It felt so good to be held. I wanted to sink into his arms, to never leave them. He stepped into the water.

"No, don't go in, there's a shark!' I struggled to be put down, but I was too weak.

He said, "It's okay, almost there," and carried me over to the boat.

I didn't really want to get in their boat, but I didn't protest as he set me down inside. His white T-shirt had dirt on it. From carrying me?

He climbed in and tucked a shiny silver blanket around me, then another guy started the boat and headed for the NOAA ship. As we moved in the waves, it felt different from being in the raft. Faster, of course. But more purposeful. Not just drifting.

The wind blew in my face as I accepted another bottle of water.

I turned to look back at the island. *Good-bye, Starbuck.*

*Good-bye, Max.*

And then I passed out.

## fifty-seven

Something soft was under my head. And something else smelled. Bad.

The back of my right hand hurt and itched at the same time. I reached over and felt tape.

I opened my eyes.

An IV tube snaked out of my hand and up into a clear bag of fluid. I squinted but couldn't read the label. My arm looked strange. Striped. Then I realized it was clean from the elbow down, dirty the rest of the way.

I was lying in a narrow bed. My headache was gone for the first time in ages.

"Welcome back." A bald guy with black glasses rolled over on a wheeled stool. "I'm Dr. Gary." He smiled. "You're in pretty good shape, considering—"

"I don't want to talk about it." The words were practically out of my mouth before I even thought them. "Sorry."

Dr. Gary shook his head slightly. "You don't have to."

My eye welled up and I wiped it with my fingers, then held them up. They glistened. "I have tears again."

"You were very dehydrated." He nodded at the IV bag. "We gave you a couple of those." He smiled. "Let's get you fixed up so you can get out of those clothes and get cleaned up."

As he snapped on gloves, I glanced down.

No wonder I'd gotten the other guy's shirt dirty. At that point, *Robie* could have been listed in the dictionary as a synonym for *filth*. That was what I smelled. I was grateful that the doctor didn't say a word. He didn't look like he was holding his breath, but he was. I heard him suck in, then not breathe in for a bit as he inspected my left eye.

"I'll give you some anti-inflammatory pills for this. It's very badly bruised. Once the swelling goes down, it should be fine." He took a look at my nose as I explained what happened.

Dr. Gary stood up. "There's some infection in there. Probably a good thing the diamond did get ripped out. I'll give you some anti-biotics. And I'd better put a couple stitches in there."

I must have made a face because he said, "I'm good. There won't be a scar."

He cleaned my nose with some pads and smelly stuff, then left the room for a minute.

The rumble of the engines increased and I felt us move. We were leaving. I shut my eyes.

When I opened them, the doctor stood there, hand poised above me, holding a syringe. "This will sting, but then you won't feel the stitches."

Without thinking, I said, "Wait. Can you tell me something worse?"

His brow furrowed as he stood there.

"Worse?"

*Worse.*

Any given day of the last ten days—ten days?—was *worse.*

Any given *minute.*

No one would ever have to tell me anything *worse,* because I'd been through worse.

I'd lived *worse.* And I had survived *worse.*

So I waved him off with a hand. "Never mind."

The shot was nothing compared to the pain when the diamond came out. And I didn't feel a single stitch.

"Do you feel like you can sit up?"

I nodded, and sat up without even feeling dizzy. "I'm really hungry."

He practically ran over to a small black refrigerator and opened it. He turned to me. "You want vanilla, chocolate, or strawberry?"

My mouth watered. "Yes."

He grinned and pulled out a couple cans, and popped the top of one. "It's a meal replacement shake. Take your time, see how your stomach adjusts to food. We can go a lot longer without food than we can without water. Do you know how long it's been?"

I shook my head and glanced at the pink label before taking a drink. Strawberry. I'd never tasted anything so amazing in my life and I wanted to guzzle it all. I finished the strawberry and opened the chocolate.

The doctor smiled. "Now that we have you on your way to recovery, we should probably find out who you are."

"I'm Robie Mitchell. I live on Midway."

"Midway Atoll?"

I nodded.

His forehead scrunched up. "I'll be right back."

He left and returned a few minutes later, holding a sheet of paper. He turned it my way so I could see the photo on it.

It was me. Taken a few months ago on Midway. "Why do you have that?"

"They sent this everywhere when you were abducted."

*What?*

*I wasn't abducted.*

He set a hand on my arm. "Your aunt declared you missing twelve days ago when her friend couldn't find you. And a couple witnesses came forward and said they saw a guy grab you near McDonald's."

Twelve days? Had it been that long?

He cocked his head a little and looked from me to the photo. "But with those little braids you don't look anything like this."

I pushed away the images of the McDonald's and the man as I shook my head. "I wasn't abducted. I was on the plane."

Dr. Gary asked, "What plane?"

"The supply flight to Midway on the twenty-first. The G-One from Oahu Air Services."

He ran a hand through his short dark hair. "Impossible." He spoke slowly, like he was trying to get me to understand. "No one survived that crash."

"I did!" Why wouldn't he listen to me? Because I was a teenager? They would listen to Max. And I started to say, "Ask Max."

But I didn't. Because if I did, I knew what they'd find. Or rather, what they wouldn't find. Max. He wasn't on the island, wasn't in the raft. And, except for the first night and day, never was. I thought he was though. I made him be there for me.

I made him be there.

I made him.

Which left me. The only one who survived the crash.

There was no one else to refute my story, verify my claims. My word, for maybe the only time in my life, would be gospel. No one had to know what I'd done. No one had to ever find out that I'd left Max.

Dr. Gary stood up. "I have to get someone to work on setting up a satellite call with Midway. We need to get hold of your folks." He came back a few minutes later. "They said it might not be until tomorrow; Midway is having some satellite trouble."

I sighed. "Typical."

"I'll let you know as soon as they get the connection. Do you want to try to stand?"

Dr. Gary held my elbow and I swayed a bit, but managed to walk with his help. He pulled the IV pole along as he led me over to a scale. He tried to keep me from seeing the numbers, but I managed to get a glimpse of the first. It was a nine.

I asked, "Can I get cleaned up?"

He frowned. "How are you feeling?"

I said, "Dirty."

He nodded. "How about a little more rest, then we'll see?"

I got back in the bed and shut my eyes, just to appease him, but fell asleep right away.

I woke up feeling refreshed and drank another shake.

Dr. Gary took all my vital signs, seemed pretty happy about them, and unhooked the IV. Then, the red-haired woman from the beach came to help. She told me her name was Kristen and she was twenty-two, in grad school. She took me to a room with two bunks, a desk and chair, and its own bathroom. "Looks like you'll be my roomie the rest of the way."

I asked, "Way to where?" I didn't want to go back to Honolulu. I didn't want to have to get on a plane to fly back to Midway. I couldn't. My heart sped up.

She smiled. "We're on our way up the chain. We should have you home in about a week."

"Home?" The word felt funny.

She nodded. "Yeah. Midway is on our schedule. How lucky is that?"

*Pretty frickin' lucky.*

She went to get me some stuff, and I stood there unsteadily, leaning against the wall, not wanting to touch anything, get something else dirty.

Kristen came back with a stack of white towels and an assortment of hotel-size shampoos and conditioners and toothpaste, then held up a red toothbrush still in its package.

I smiled and reached out to take the towels.

"Why don't you just hop in that shower first? I'll get rid of your clothes." She glanced at them. "Do you want me to wash them?" She looked skeptical.

I shook my head. "I never want to see them again."

"There's someone your size, I'll see what I can round up. We all bring extras with us. Not much shopping out here." She took everything in the bathroom. I heard the shower start. She came back out. "Just toss your clothes out once you're in."

I stood there, not moving.

"Do you need some help, Robie?"

How long had it been since I heard someone say my name? I swallowed. A tear ran down my cheek. "I didn't think I would ever feel safe again."

Kristen stepped forward and hugged me. I held on tight. She smelled so nice, I was embarrassed at how I must have smelled. But she didn't stop hugging until I stepped back.

She asked, "You okay?"

I nodded and went into the bathroom. I peeled off my clothes, dropping them in a heap, then stepped into the shower.

Even though the shower was probably standard for a NOAA research vessel, sort of tinny and small, I was so happy to be in it. The pitiful stream of water was hot at least and drizzled past my skin and into my soul. I stood there forever before I even made a move to soap up.

I used all four little bottles of body wash and three washcloths before I was done. The first washcloth was nearly black, the second was gray, and finally, the third was actually still white when I'd finished. And then I washed my tangled hair three times.

The water was threatening to cool by the end, and that was my cue to get out. Reluctantly, I stepped out onto the rubber bathmat. I dried off, relishing how hot and steamy my body felt. *How clean.*

My clothes were gone.

A pile of different ones lay on the stainless steel vanity next to the toothbrush. Ignoring them, I stood there in my towel and brushed my teeth so many times I emptied the little tube of toothpaste. I couldn't stop running my tongue over my teeth, they were so smooth. Then I finished drying off and turned to the clothes.

On top was a navy blue long-sleeve T-shirt with NOAA in white letters on the front. Underneath it was a sports bra that looked brand-new and a pair of pink underwear with the price tag on. Below that was a pair of black sweatpants. I dressed quickly, loving the feel of the fresh, soft clothes against my clean skin, even though the clothes were a bit too big. My stomach growled.

A voice came through the closed door. "Are you ready to go to dinner?"

Kristen. She must have been waiting the whole time.

I opened the door.

She smiled. "You look so much better."

"I feel so much better." I laid a hand on my stomach. "But I'm starving."

"Then let's go eat."

The next morning, I woke up between warm sheets that smelled of springtime. Stretching out my legs and arms, I yawned with a pleased groan, loving the feel of the soft bed beneath me. I ran my hands through my soft, clean hair. It took two hours, most of which I dozed through, but Kristen and another woman took out my cornrows, and then I washed my hair for the fourth time. It was a little thinner than before, but I figured a properly placed ponytail would cover up the bald spot.

But that had all happened after I ate. Dinner was in my bed. Even though I was dying for a cheeseburger and fries, Dr. Gary told me plain food might be better than something richer. Kristen brought me cheese and bread and a sliced orange, and I was stuffed before finishing half of my plate. My stomach had shrunk a lot, I guess.

But after a good night's sleep, I was ready to eat again.

I sat up and reached for one of the four full water bottles sitting on my bedside table. I downed almost half of it, then opened the top drawer just long enough to view the pile of granola bars Kristen had put there last night. I closed it again.

*Still there.*

Someone knocked on my door. I had been woken up twice in the night so the doctor could check my vital signs, but had gone right back to sleep both times. I'd slept in just the T-shirt, so I quickly threw on the sweatpants.

Kristen stood there. "Good morning! You look so much better."

I nodded as I yawned again. "I feel better."

"Midway got their satellite up and your parents know you're safe. As soon as you're ready, we can call again and you can talk to them yourself."

Barefoot, I followed her up to the bridge, trying not to run even though I could hardly contain myself. I just wanted to talk to my mom and my dad. The last twelve hours had seemed just as unreal as the first twelve hours after the G-1 crashed. I needed something to prove that I was off the island. That I really was saved.

The bridge was a huge room with large windows that looked out onto the ocean. Nothing but water. I turned away.

Kristen said, "Joe here will take care of you." She squeezed my shoulder and left.

Joe was tall and thin and had a nice smile. He did a couple things and handed me the phone.

Reception was fuzzy and cut out now and then, but I heard the ring on the other end. My heart pounded and my hands shook so hard, I almost dropped the phone.

*Click.*

The voice was breathless and anxious. "Hello?"

"Mommy!" It was the only word I got out.

"Robie, thank God!"

And then I could do nothing but sob and gulp for air as I listened to my mom on the other end, telling me, "It's okay. It's okay."

I believed her.

And when it was time to hang up, I still hadn't said anything else. Joe took the phone from me and put an arm around me. "Everything is going to be okay."

I decided to believe him too.

# Epilogue

We are less than a day from docking at Midway. I'm so excited, I couldn't even sleep last night. Although it's been hard to wait, the past week on the ship has been almost fun.

People keep giving me things, and I have a whole pile of T-shirts and hats and beauty products. We've been watching movies and playing video games. And eating. I've been eating a lot. Not enough that I get rid of my stash in the bedside table though. When I get down to one granola bar, I go to the dining room and get more. Just to be sure.

I'm packing all the things in my new NOAA duffel when there's a knock on the door. I open it to see Brian, the original guy from the beach. He says, "We have your stuff for you. I didn't want you to forget it."

I glance over at the bed, at all the stuff I'm trying to pack into the duffel. "What stuff?"

He gestures behind him. "From the island. The stuff we found by the raft and on the dune by your campfire. We assumed you'd want it."

I breathe in, shuddering a little. Did I want any of it? Did I want to be reminded?

"Want to at least look?" He must see my hesitation. "We can get rid of it if you want." He grins. "There are a lot of takers for that glass ball."

I nod. "I'll look." I slip on a pair of white flip-flops someone gave me.

He leads me up to a storage room of some sort, with metal bins and boxes.

I walk in and stop. The raft is there on the floor, folded up. It looks so small.

"Here." He points to a table where I see the glass ball. And the Santa Claus. And Max's ditty bag.

"The glass ball and Santa are mine." I swallow. "But the bag isn't."

Brian turns to me. "Whose is it?"

"Max's." I swallow. "Max . . . Cameron. The copilot."

His eyes narrow. "The one who died in the crash?"

I haven't told anyone anything about the crash. They only know what they hear. "He didn't die in the crash."

With a whistle, Brian sucks in a breath and sits down on a bin. "Are you serious?"

I nod. "He saved me though. Got me into the raft."

He looks at the raft. "It's really ripped up."

The picture of that day, that moment, jumps into my head and I can't speak.

He shakes his head. "You were lucky to survive all that, you know."

"I know." I open Max's bag. "Do you think someone will want the manifest?"

He nods. "Probably. I assume they're going to ask you a lot of questions."

"I figured that." I sigh.

He glances at his watch. "I'll be back in a few minutes. You okay by yourself?"

"Yeah." I watch him go, then step over to the raft. I push the edge with my flip-flop and the rubber rustles. The raft is airless. Lifeless. It has nothing left.

Is it even a raft anymore? Or just colored rubber?

I squat down beside the raft and grasp an edge.

How many hours had I sat in that thing, hoping? Hoping to be rescued?

And Max. The raft was the last place he'd been alive. The place he'd spoken his last word. And I'd been the only one there to hear it.

I pick up the ditty bag, reach inside, and pull out the spiral notebook. I sit down, cross my legs, and turn to the last few unread pages, the last time Max would speak to me.

*Brandy's mother blamed me. Why wouldn't she? She didn't want me at the funeral. I had to wait until it was over, until the service at the cemetery was done. I went there after dark, kneeled beside the fresh mound of dirt. There wasn't a headstone yet, just that pile of earth. I put my face in it. My tears turned some of it to mud.*

*I stayed there until the sun came up.*

*I enlisted in the National Guard the next day. I needed out of there. Not just college. Somewhere farther. A few weeks later, I was packed, ready to leave. A car pulled in the driveway and the doorbell rang. I answered it, and discovered the art teacher standing there. I didn't even know her name. I never took art.*

*She smiled and handed me a small velvet pouch. She said it was Brandy's. There was a small card with my name.*

*I pulled open the drawstring and stuck my finger in. I pulled out a black cord, on the end of which dangled an oblong piece of silver. A pattern of black swirls covered one side and I held it closer. A thumbprint.*

*Reflexively, I held it to my lips, then felt her looking at me. I lowered it. It was beautiful.*

*The teacher reached for the necklace. I handed it to her. She turned it over and showed me the blank side. Then she explained that Brandy had meant to add my thumbprint.*

*My vision blurred and I realized I was crying. I held the necklace to my heart.*

*And that's why I wear it. It's all I have left of her. It makes me feel like she's still with me. Like a little part of her soul is still hanging on.*

I'm all choked up, and I swallow. I close the cover of the spiral notebook and, for the last time, read the magic marker note scrawled on the cover.

*Max Cameron: Therapy Journal*

I stuff it back into the ditty bag. Then and there, I decide to contact Max's family, give this to them. Tell them that Max saved my life. And not just when he pulled me out of the water.

I start to get up. Then I notice something nestled in the creases of the raft.

I reach out . . .

. . . and pick up the black cord, the silver thumbprint dangling in the air.

My breath is a choke, a sob.

Impossible.

*Impossible.*

The necklace had never been off Max. *He had never taken it off.*

"It can't be real."

I fold my hand around the silver and it's warm. From my touch?

"Max."

I open my hand and turn the silver over to the blank side. But it's not blank. There's a thumbprint there as well. I put my thumb over it, but it's much bigger than the other. It's the size of a man's thumbprint.

*Max?*

I put a hand over my eyes and sit there, clutching the necklace.

Someone knocks on the door and I jump up, holding my fist with the necklace to my chest.

A guy pokes his head in. "About two hours to Midway."

I kind of smile and nod. Then I lift the glass ball into my arms and cradle it, ignoring the salty, mildewed scent of fish and sea and old barnacles.

He starts to leave, then says, "You okay, alone in here?"

He leaves once I assure him I am okay.

Because I'm not alone.

I open my hand and look at the necklace.

At least I think I'm not alone.

Maybe I never was.

## MY THANKS GO OUT TO:

My agent, Scott Mendel, and my editor, Liz Szabla. Without them, this book wouldn't have happened. Seriously.

All the wonderful people at Feiwel and Friends/Macmillan who spend time and effort on behalf of me and my books. I am so grateful.

Matt Jaeger, for always telling me the truth about my words, especially when I don't want to hear it.

Tracy Bodeen Wachtler, for her firsthand description of body piercing, so I didn't have to take my research down a painful path.

Stephanie Boman, for providing me with a mountain cabin retreat, where I pounded out the first 10,000 words of the draft, complete with Skittle counting.

Karen Dinsmore, for patiently listening to me ramble on about pointless plot lines for miles, literally.

The Thompsons and the Becks, for making me realize I can always find fun people to hang out with, even in the desolate high desert of Eastern Oregon.

Maranda Robbins, owner of the fabulous indie bookstore The Book Parlor, in Burns, Oregon, for being so supportive of my books.

Finally, this book could not have been written unless I had happened to live on a remote Pacific atoll, an experience I owe to my husband, as well as our two smart and beautiful daughters, who made that adventure an unforgettable family affair. This book is my somewhat-twisted love letter to Midway, a place that stole my heart the moment I stepped off of the G-1. (Which, lucky for me, never crashed when I was on it.)

Thank you for reading
this FEIWEL AND FRIENDS book.

The Friends who made

# THE
# RAFT

possible are:

**Jean Feiwel**, publisher
**Liz Szabla**, editor-in-chief
**Rich Deas**, creative director
**Elizabeth Fithian**, marketing director
**Holly West**, assistant to the publisher
**Dave Barrett**, managing editor
**Lauren A. Burniac**, associate editor
**Nicole Liebowitz Moulaison**, production manager
**Ksenia Winnicki**, publishing associate
**Anna Roberto**, editorial assistant

Find out more about our authors and artists
and our future publishing at
macteenbooks.com.

OUR BOOKS ARE FRIENDS FOR LIFE

DATE DUE